JIM ELDRIDGE

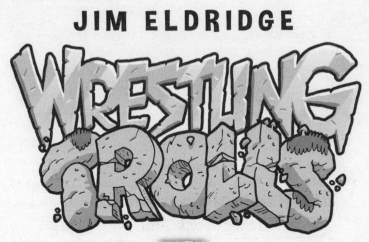

MATCH 3

THE GIANT RUMBLE

Illustrated by JAN BIELECKI

HOT KEY BOOKS

First published in Great Britain in 2014 by Hot Key Books
Northburgh House, 10 Northburgh Street, London EC1V 0AT

Text © Jim Eldridge 2014
Illustrations © Jan Bielecki 2014

A CIP catalogue record for this book is available from the British Library.

ISBN: 978-1-4714-0263-0

1

This book is typeset in 11pt Sabon using Atomik ePublisher

Printed and bound by Clays Ltd, St Ives Plc

To all those who took part in The Wrestling Trolls Story Adventure. This story is yours

Chapter One

From their dressing room at the back of the packed arena, Jack could hear the audience shouting.

'Orcs! Orcs! Orcs!' chanted some of the crowd, while others yelled out, 'Big Rock,' and still others, 'We love the Masked Avenger!'

'They are cheering louder for you two,' Jack declared to his friends.

Tonight, Big Rock and the Masked Avenger were taking on two of the villainous Lord Veto's Wrestling Orcs: Smash and Squirm.

'Stand still!' instructed Meenu, as she made a last adjustment to the Masked Avenger's full head-mask.

'Sorry,' replied Princess Ava. 'I'm just ready to

take on those orcs.'

The Masked Avenger was actually the young Princess Ava from the Kingdom of Weevil. The challenge was that her mask could only be removed and her identity revealed, if she was beaten in the ring. So far, she was unbeaten.

'There,' said Meenu, at last. 'That shouldn't come off, no matter what the orcs do to it.'

'Unless they win,' commented Robin the old horse, drily.

'They won't,' promised Big Rock.

'But these are orcs,' said Jack, worried. 'They cheat.'

'They won't beat me and Masked Avenger,' said Big Rock confidently. 'We good tag team.'

'No, you two are a *great* tag team,' corrected Milo.

Thirteen-year-old Milo was the manager of Waldo's Wrestling Trolls, or WWT for short. Not long ago, ten-year-old Jack had earned his place as the assistant trainer, and Robin, the horse who pulled their caravan, seemed like he'd been around forever. Along with Meenu, the girl from Weevil who designed Princess Ava's outfits – both the princess dresses she had to wear and the wrestling costumes she chose to wear – Jack, Milo and Robin were the support for the tag team duo: Big Rock and the Masked Avenger.

Milo cocked his head to one side as the noise from the arena grew suddenly louder – whistles and stamping of thousands of feet.

'Sounds like the orcs have just come in,' he said. 'Time for us to go. You two ready?'

'Never better!' said Princess Ava, and she and Big Rock slapped palms. Jack noticed that Big Rock didn't slap too hard. A knock from the giant Big Rock could put a hole in a wall.

'Okay,' said Milo. 'Let's go!'

Milo opened the door, and Big Rock and the Masked Avenger stepped out into the aisle. As they started towards the ring a huge roar of applause went up, mixed with some loud booing from the orcs' supporters.

The lights bounced off Big Rock's granite body and his wrestling costume: a multicoloured spangly outfit with a picture of a mountain-top on the front.

The Masked Avenger looked tiny beside him in her red leotard beneath her purple cloak.

The two orcs were already in the ring, dressed identically in black-and-white costumes with a red lightning flash on the front.

'You know, I've never seen Ava – er, the Masked Avenger wrestle before,' Meenu whispered to Jack.

'You're in for a treat,' Jack whispered back. It hadn't been that long ago that Jack had been forbidden to watch wrestling matches, and he never tired of the excitement.

They reached the ring and Big Rock and the Masked Avenger pulled themselves up and through the ropes. The two orcs snarled and sneered, and Smash glowered at the pair with his blood-red eyes as he snapped the sharp claws of his talons together, making sparks fly off them.

Milo, Jack, Meenu and Robin took their places beneath Big Rock and the Avenger's corner as the referee strode to the centre of the ring.

'My lord, ladies and gentlemen!' he boomed. 'Welcome to the main bout of the evening, a tag contest between Big Rock and the Masked Avenger, and that incredible Wrestling Orc duo, Smash and Squirm!

'The rules,' he continued. 'Only one member of each team in the ring at a time, the other outside, holding the tag rope. The one outside can only enter the ring and take over when their partner has tagged them by touching them with their hand. Clear?'

Everyone grunted, and the Masked Avenger cracked her knuckles.

'Let the contest begin!' the referee shouted.

Big Rock took his position on the apron of the ring outside the ropes, while in the other corner, Squirm gripped his tag rope and watched his orc partner, Smash, circle the tiny figure of the Masked Avenger.

Smash made his first move, leaping at the Masked Avenger and kicking both legs at her in a drop kick.

The Masked Avenger dodged to one side. Smash was obviously expecting this, because as he landed he lashed out at her ankles with his sharp claws. But the Masked Avenger had second-guessed him, and she leapt into the air and then came down, landing with both feet on his arm.

Before the orc realised what was happening, the Masked Avenger had grabbed Smash's other arm and turned the orc onto his face.

WHAM!

The Masked Avenger dropped on the orc's back, driving Smash's sharp beak through the canvas of the ring. Trapped, the orc struggled to push himself up, but as he did so the Masked Avenger flipped him over onto his back, and then brought both her legs down on his chest and arms, forcing his shoulders to the canvas.

'One!' shouted the crowd excitedly.

'Two,' said the referee. 'Three!'

The crowd went wild as the Masked Avenger rolled off the fallen orc and bounced to the ropes, where Big Rock was waiting.

'Good fall,' smiled Big Rock, as he and Princess Ava touched hands, tagging Big Rock to take her place in the ring.

At the ringside, Jack gave Meenu a high five.

'First fall to our team,' grinned Milo. 'One more fall or a knockout, and it's victory to us!'

But Jack had spotted a dreaded figure across the arena. He gestured to the back of the hall where Lord Veto, the owner of the Wrestling Orcs, was in deep conversation with Warg, his Chief Orc.

'Those two are up to something,' muttered Jack. 'I'm going to find out what.'

As Jack pushed his way through the crowd, in the ring, Big Rock faced up to Squirm. The two threw themselves at one another, and the whole arena seemed to shake as they crunched together, with bits of quartz flying off Big Rock's body as Squirm raked the troll with his talons.

'Those idiots are losing,' Jack heard Lord Veto hiss to Warg as he got nearer.

'It's only one fall so far, my Lord,' responded Warg.

'I don't care! I can't take the chance on our team losing in front of all these people.' Then Lord Veto leaned closer to Warg and began to whisper in his ear. The orc listened, then nodded and slid away, out of the hall.

Jack hurried back to the others.

'Lord Veto's definitely up to something,' he said.

'What?' asked Milo.

'I don't know,' admitted Jack. 'But one thing's for sure, if Lord Veto's involved it will be sneaky and rotten.'

'Shush,' said Robin. 'I'm trying to watch the match.'

In the ring, Big Rock had Squirm in a bear hug, but the orc managed to wriggle out, squeezing himself upwards.

Then the orc hauled himself up onto the giant troll's shoulders. An elbow from Squirm caught Big Rock in the eye, then he grabbed Big Rock round the head, with both clawed hands locking together.

The orc threw himself backwards, intending

to make the big troll fall. Instead, Big Rock stood his ground; then he reached up, snatched Squirm off his head and threw him at the corner post.

WHUMP!!!

Squirm hit the corner post and bounced back into the ring, and as he did Big Rock fell on him, pinning both his shoulders to the canvas.

'A pinfall!' yelled Milo delightedly. 'One . . .'

Before he and the referee could take up the count, there was a sudden massive surge from the crowd, and the next moment what looked like a small army of Wrestling Orcs, all dressed in identical costumes to Smash and Squirm, had invaded the ring.

As the crowd roared – some in loud disapproval, some in support of the orcs – the referee tried in vain to intervene, but it was no use. The orcs had taken over. About five orcs had rushed to Squirm's aid, leaping on Big Rock and punching and kicking at him.

Furious at this, the Masked Avenger let go of her tag rope and leapt into the ring to go to

Big Rock's rescue, but it was obvious to everyone that she and the troll were hopelessly outnumbered. The orcs were already piling onto the Masked Avenger, dragging her down to the canvas.

'She's going to get stomped!' gasped the horrified Meenu. 'They're both going to get crushed!'

Jack felt a sense of deep anger and injustice rise in him as he watched what was happening in the ring, and his eyes began to fill up with tears. No, not with tears, with a sort of . . . mist. Like thick, opaque crystals forming. And, at the same time, he felt a shuddering sensation course through him.

'GRAAAARRR!'

The roar was so loud it sent shock waves around the whole arena. It made the orcs in the ring stop their pounding of Big Rock and the Masked Avenger and look to see where the massive sound came from.

It came from a troll. And not just any troll, but a massive and very angry troll, who leapt

into the ring and began to pick up orcs with his huge hands and throw them out of the ring as if they were dolls. Soon the area outside the ring was littered with Wrestling Orcs, moaning and groaning.

The referee had managed to get back into the ring. As Big Rock and the Masked Avenger lurched to their feet, the referee announced: 'Ladies and gentlemen! Because of the invasion of the ring, I regret to tell you that this bout has been rendered null and void. It's cancelled!'

At this there was a huge shouting of disapproval, with boos ringing around the arena.

Big Rock and Princess Ava clambered out of the ring and joined the gang. Both looked glum.

'We were winning,' grunted Big Rock.

'Jack was right!' fumed Milo. 'Lord Veto did this!' Milo stomped off towards the referee.

'And nearly got us flattened by those orcs,' sighed Princess Ava/the Masked Avenger.

'You were lucky that big troll appeared,' said Meenu. 'Where did he go? And where did he come from? I never saw him before that.'

'Actually, that was Jack,' said Princess Ava.

Meenu, puzzled, looked at the small, thin – almost fragile – figure of Jack.

'You mean it was a friend of his?'

'No, it was Jack,' repeated Ava.

Meenu looked at Jack, and then laughed. 'Yeah, right!' she chuckled.

'It true,' said Big Rock. 'Jack half-troll.'

'When he gets angry, his inner troll comes out and he turns into Thud,' explained Ava.

'Thud?'

'It's who he becomes when his troll side comes out.'

'I thought of that name,' said Robin proudly.

Meenu looked at Jack, stunned. The small boy gave an embarrassed smile.

Meenu smiled. 'That was so *cool*!'

The sound of angry shouting from the other side of the ring interrupted them.

'That's Milo!' said Big Rock.

They hurried round the ring and found Milo and Lord Veto nose to nose in anger, although Milo had to stand on tiptoe to achieve it.

'You are a cheat!' yelled Milo. 'You knew you were being beaten so you fixed that invasion!'

'Me, a cheat?' shouted back Lord Veto. 'What about that freak troll of yours? He damaged five of my precious orcs! I've a good mind to sue you for damages!'

Lord Veto looked around, puzzled. 'Where did he go, anyway?'

'Never mind him,' raged Milo. 'You and your cheating orcs have no place in wrestling!'

'That's right.' Robin nodded. 'You make a clean game dirty.'

'Shut up!' snarled Lord Veto at the old horse.

'Utter one more word and we'll be eating horsemeat for dinner.'

'Don't you dare threaten Robin!' snapped Jack, his face glowing red with fury.

Princess Ava, Meenu and Big Rock exchanged worried looks. Was Jack so angry he was about to turn into Thud? But the moment passed. Instead, Milo glared at Lord Veto and declared loudly, 'Wrestling isn't big enough for both of us!'

At this, an evil light came into Lord Veto's eyes and a nasty smile appeared on his lips.

'No,' he said. 'I agree. So let's settle this once and for all.'

Jack, worried and suspicious about Lord Veto's manner, tried to intervene. 'Milo . . .' he began.

But Milo ignored him. 'Come on, then!' he demanded. 'What's your challenge?'

'A Giant Rumble,' said Lord Veto. 'Ten of my Wrestling Orcs against ten of your Wrestling Trolls, in the ring together. Last one standing is the winner. The loser will withdraw his team from the Wrestling Federation, which means they cannot enter any tournaments ever again.'

'Done!' nodded Milo.

Jack gasped.

Lord Veto smiled. 'Yes,' he said with a silky smile. 'I think you have been.' He turned to his Chief Orc. 'Come, Warg. We have a Giant Rumble to prepare for.'

With that, Lord Veto and Warg walked off.

'Ha!' said Milo defiantly. 'That told him!'

'Yes, it told him you're an idiot,' snorted Robin.

'What do you mean?' demanded Milo indignantly.

'You took a challenge to put ten Wrestling Trolls into a ring against ten of his orcs,' said Robin. 'How many Wrestling Trolls have you got?'

'Er . . .' began Milo.

'Me,' said Big Rock proudly.

'That's one,' said Robin. 'Where are you going to get the other nine?'

Meenu pointed at Jack.

'He turns into one,' she said. 'That's two.'

'But not all the time,' sighed Jack sadly. 'I can't control when it happens. It may not.'

'Let's be positive,' said Princess Ava. 'I'll annoy you in some way to make you change. So that's two.'

'There's Grit!' said Milo. 'She's a great wrestler! And she's a troll!'

'Yes, but she went off on her travels and no one knows where she is,' said Robin.

'We'll find her,' said Milo confidently. 'We'll send out carrier pigeons with messages.'

Robin gave a doubtful snort. 'It's all a bit iffy, if you ask me,' he said.

'We have to make it work,' said Big Rock firmly.

'Big Rock's right,' nodded Jack. 'Okay, finding seven more Wrestling Trolls is going to be hard –'

'More like impossible,' snorted Robin.

'But,' continued Jack firmly, ignoring the old horse's interruption, 'that's what we'll do.'

'Jack right,' nodded Big Rock. 'We do this together.'

'I can be an Honorary Troll!' blurted out Princess Ava.

'An Honorary Troll?' repeated Big Rock, puzzled.

'Yes, it means I can be . . . a Wrestling Troll for the occasion,' said Princess Ava.

'Big Rock, Grit, the Masked Avenger and me – if I can turn into Thud,' said Jack, counting on his fingers. 'That's four.'

'Hmm. It *could* work,' said Robin. 'But we still need another six.'

'Then we'll find six more Wrestling Trolls and put together a team,' declared Milo.

'And where,' enquired Robin, 'are we going to find them?'

'We'll use my Uncle Waldo's map,' said Milo. 'The one he marked up with all the places he took Waldo's Wrestling Trolls to. We're bound to find some good wrestlers there.' He gave a confident grin. 'Let's go get the map! We're going on a journey!'

As Milo, Big Rock and Jack headed for the dressing room, Meenu looked at Ava excitedly. 'This is great!' she whispered. 'It'll be just like my family's holiday road trips – all working together.'

'Yes, it will.' Ava smiled.

The two girls headed after the others, with Robin following.

'A family,' said Robin quietly to himself. 'I like that.'

Chapter Two

The battered caravan trundled along through the Wind Swept Park. Milo was driving, which meant that he sat on the seat at the front and held the reins, while Robin pulled the caravan at a speed of his choosing.

Jack set next to Milo, Waldo's old map open on his lap.

Big Rock ran alongside, practising jumps and kicks and throwing air-punches.

Princess Ava and Meenu sat on the roof of the caravan, complaining as they brushed cobwebs away.

'You should have warned us we'd be going through a whole forest-load of cobwebs,' said Ava, very annoyed.

'It's not my fault,' said Jack. He tapped the map. 'It just said here we were going through Lost Woods. It didn't say anything about any cobwebs hanging down from the branches of the trees.'

'Well you should write it on the map,' said Meenu, getting the last of the cobwebs out of her hair. 'You can call it the Creepy Cobwebs Path.'

'You didn't have to ride on the roof of the caravan,' Milo pointed out. 'You both could have gone inside.'

'No we couldn't,' said Princess Ava. 'For one thing, we prefer being out in the fresh air –'

'And cobwebs,' snickered Robin.

'And, for another, the caravan is absolutely filled with so much stuff, there's hardly any room to get in it!'

'Yes,' added Meenu. 'Surely we don't need all this stuff?'

'We're going on a Quest,' said Milo. 'We need provisions.'

'Provisions are one thing,' snorted Ava, 'but

the stuff you've got inside there . . . half of it's unnecessary!'

She began to tick things off on her fingers. 'Horse treats –'

'Horse treats are vital!' said Robin firmly.

'Punch bags,' continued Princess Ava. 'A toolbox, a telescope, torches, wet wipes, make-up, dumb-bells, wrestling outfits, blankets, duvets . . .'

'And sleeping bags,' added Meenu. 'Why do you need sleeping bags when you've already got blankets and duvets?'

'It can get cold when you're on the road,' said Milo wisely.

'Lamps,' continued Princess Ava. 'Fake tan, Mighty Man Shaving Cream and Deodorant set, lavender room spray . . .'

'Cameras,' said Meenu. 'Compasses, sunglasses, toilet rolls . . .'

'Toilet rolls very important,' nodded Big Rock as he ran past, swinging punches.

'A pair of folding chairs with cup holders,' continued Meenu. 'And whose is that little teddy bear?'

'Little Bob is not just any old teddy bear!' said Jack defensively.

'Packs of cards,' added Ava, still ticking them off on her fingers, but by now she had run out of fingers. 'Boxes of games, spare pants, rolls of rope . . .'

'And where did the peace flag come from?' asked Meenu.

'That's a long story,' said Milo.

'*Far* too long,' said Robin. He stopped.

'What's that ahead?' he asked.

They all looked. The road suddenly stopped at a narrow wooden bridge.

'According to the map, that is Billy Goat Bridge,' said Jack.

'That must be why there's a very large billy goat standing in front of it, barring our way,' said Milo.

'Billy goats don't like trolls,' muttered Big Rock unhappily.

'Why not?' asked Meenu.

Big Rock shook his head. 'Don't know,' he

said. 'Billy goats make up story about trolls
eating goats. It not true. Trolls eat rocks.'

'Well, let's see what this billy goat has to say
to us,' said Milo.

Robin ambled on towards the bridge, but as
they drew near they saw that the big billy goat
had no intention of moving to let them cross.
Instead, he spread himself so that he blocked
the way across the bridge completely, forcing
the caravan to stop.

'Good day!' greeted Milo with a broad smile. 'I wonder if we might trouble you to move to one side so that we can pass over the bridge?'

'No trouble at all,' said the goat. Then he gave a nasty smile and added: 'If you pay the toll.'

'What toll?' asked Milo.

'The fee to get over the bridge,' said the goat. 'It's normally five gold pieces, but as you've got a troll with you . . .' the goat sneered as he said the word, 'it will cost you twenty pieces of gold.'

'I'm afraid we haven't got twenty pieces of gold,' said Milo. 'In fact, we haven't got any money at all. But we will have once we win the Giant Rumble.' He gestured at the big letters WWT on the side of the caravan. 'We are Waldo's Wrestling Trolls and we're on a Quest to gather ten Wrestling Trolls for a tournament.'

The goat shook his shaggy head. 'If you don't have the gold, you don't cross this bridge.'

Milo looked at the goat, then he shrugged. 'Okay,' he said. 'We don't need your bridge.

We'll find another one.'

'Actually, there isn't another one,' said Jack.

'What?' asked Milo.

Jack showed him the map. 'This is the only bridge across this river for miles and miles,' he said. 'It will take us days to find another one.'

'And that's time we don't have,' said Ava. 'Remember, we've got a tournament to get to.'

Milo sighed. He turned back to the goat.

'Look, how about if I give you an IOU,' he said. 'We'll owe you the money, and when we've won the Giant Rumble, we'll come back and pay you.'

Again, the goat shook his head. 'No,' he said. 'We don't trust wrestlers, and we especially don't trust trolls.'

'How about royalty?' asked Ava, and she jumped down from the roof of the caravan and approached the goat, standing as tall as she could and looking very regal, despite the traces of cobwebs in her hair. 'I am Princess Ava of the Kingdom of Weevil, and I have enough gold in the royal coffers to be able to pay your toll to get across this bridge.'

'Do you have the gold on you?' asked the goat.

'Well, no,' said Ava. 'Like I said, it's in the royal coffers in my kingdom.'

'Royalty don't carry gold around with them,' added Meenu.

'Well, when you get it out of your royal coffers and bring it here, *then* you can cross over the bridge,' sneered the goat.

'This is ridiculous!' snapped Milo. 'We're wasting time. Big Rock, pick this goat up and throw it to one side so we can get on.'

Big Rock shook his head. 'Not good idea,' he said. 'Goats say we trolls are brutes. If I do that, they say that proof we trolls bad people.'

'You *are* bad people,' said the goat. 'You trolls eat goats!'

'I never eat goat, ever,' protested Big Rock.

'I've had enough of this!' snorted Milo. 'Robin, move on and knock this goat to one side. He can't stop us. After all, there are all of us against just one goat.'

'Er . . . lots of goats,' said Jack unhappily.

About twenty more goats had suddenly appeared from under the bridge and from behind trees.

'Uh-oh,' muttered Robin.

As the goats began to circle out and surround the caravan, Meenu whispered, 'I think the time has come for us to make a tactical retreat.'

'It's too late for that,' said the big billy goat. 'You threatened us. For that, you're going to have to pay a fine, as well as the toll!'

'You're just a bunch of crooks,' said Jack accusingly. 'This is robbery!'

'And we've already told you we don't have any money,' said Milo.

'Then I suggest you get some,' smiled the goat. 'Because you're going to need it to pay the ransom to free the troll.'

Jack stared at the goat, puzzled.

'But he's already free,' he said.

'Not for much longer,' smiled the goat.

And then, before the gang knew what was happening, all the goats had turned their backs on them and . . .

'Goat farts!' shouted Princess Ava in warning, and they desperately tried to cover their mouths and noses, but it was too late. As the noxious fumes hit them and enveloped them, they tumbled to the ground, unconscious.

Chapter Three

Jack opened his eyes. His head felt fuzzy. He realised he was lying on the grass. He sat up, and he was aware that he still had the smell of goats in his nostrils.

The others were also waking up: Milo, Ava, Meenu and Robin. But there was no sign of Big Rock.

The big billy goat called out, 'We've hidden the troll somewhere safe. If you try and attack us, he will come to harm.'

About ten goats were standing across Billy Goat Bridge. The big billy goat was in front of them, and on a chain attached to one of his horns Jack saw that he had a phoenix, its hollow eyes glaring at them.

'If you hurt Big Rock, you will pay for it!' shouted Milo.

'No, the ones who are going to be paying are *you*,' said the goat. 'With gold.'

Ava whispered to Milo, 'We can't fight them. They've got a phoenix!'

Robin nodded. 'Phoenixes can be deadly. You never know what they will turn into.'

'But we've got to get past them to get to Big Rock,' said Jack.

'I know!' said Meenu brightly. 'Limericks!'
The others stared at her.

'Limericks?' echoed Milo.

'Yes!' said Ava. 'It's something Meenu and I used to do to try and make each other laugh. If we can get the goats to laugh . . .'

'Great idea!' said Jack.

'Well?' demanded the big billy goat. 'What have you got to say?'

Meenu smiled and sang,

'Robin's the name of a horse.
He was very greedy of course
He ate all the snacks
That Milo had packed
And on them he poured lots of sauce.'

At this, one of the goats began to chuckle. 'Good one!' he laughed. 'Can you come up with an answer to that, old horse?'

'Don't talk to them!' ordered the big billy goat.

But Robin nodded his head, and said,

'There once was a horse called Rob,
Who would take on any large mob.
He was a trustworthy steed
But not built for speed
But still did a very good job.'

At this, the goats chuckled louder, and Jack thought he even saw the mouth of the big billy goat twitch.

'I've got one!' said Milo.

'There once was a wrestling pack,
Big Rock, Ava, Meenu, Robin and Jack.
The evil Lord Veto,
They wanted to beat-o
But will goat farts make them turn back?'

That did it. The next moment the goats were laughing helplessly, rolling about on the bridge. Even the big billy goat was laughing out loud so much that he fell over.

'Quick!' shouted Milo. 'Over the bridge!'

Milo, Ava and Meenu leapt on board the caravan as Robin hauled it over the bridge, past the helpless goats, who were rolling about, still laughing.

'Come on, Jack!' yelled Milo.

'Wait!' said Jack.

He was watching the phoenix. Jack saw that the hollowness in the beautiful creature's eyes wasn't because it was scary and angry; it was

there because the bird was miserable.

Jack dodged one goat's horns and jumped over another's. While the big billy goat was still guffawing, Jack grabbed at the chain around the phoenix's neck. He found a catch, and clicked it open.

The phoenix let out a cry, spread its wings, and flew upwards.

'Come on, Jack!' yelled Milo again.

'Nooo!' shouted the big billy goat.

Jack ran back over the bridge as the goats began to recover and give chase.

He jumped towards the caravan and Ava and Meenu hauled him on board.

'Run for it, Robin!' urged Milo.

'At my age?' complained the horse, but he did the best he could, running as fast as was possible.

'We still don't know where the goats have got Big Rock,' pointed out Ava.

'Wherever it is, it's on this side of the bridge,' said Milo. 'We just have to look.'

Suddenly a shadow fell over them, and they

looked up to see the phoenix hurtling down towards them.

'Look out!' called Milo in alarm. 'They've set the phoenix on us!'

Instead, the phoenix landed on the roof of the caravan beside them.

'Thank you,' it said to Jack. 'My name is Blaze. I have been trying to escape from those goats for a long time, but even with my fire I couldn't break that chain.' The phoenix then turned to Milo and said, 'Your friend is being held in the Deep Dark Woods. That's where the goats keep all their prisoners –'

'I hate to interrupt,' said Robin, 'but we've got trouble.'

The goats were closing in on them fast.

'If only we could get to Big Rock,' groaned Jack.

'You can,' said the phoenix. 'You set me free. I will carry you to the Deep Dark Woods on my back.'

'But I'll be too heavy for you,' said Jack, who was the same size as the phoenix.

'Not if I change,' replied the phoenix. And then, before their eyes, there was a flash and in the phoenix's place was a large green dragon.

'Wow!' said Meenu. 'That is so cool!'

'Quick!' said the phoenix. 'Jump on my back!'

Jack did, and almost before he'd had a chance to get a firm grip, the dragon had risen into the air.

'Hold tight!' said the phoenix-dragon.

'I'm trying,' said Jack.

He gripped the dragon's neck and they soared up, and then flew off.

Jack looked back to see that the goats had caught up with the caravan, and were leaping up at it while Milo, Ava, Meenu and Robin did their best to fight them off.

'Please let them get away,' wished Jack. 'Please!'

Jack and the phoenix-dragon flew lower and lower over the huge green canopy of leaves covering an enormous wood, landing on a large rock. As soon as Jack had jumped down from its back, it changed into a phoenix again.

'From here, we're on foot,' whispered the phoenix. 'The goat camp is just ahead.'

As they crept through the undergrowth, they could hear the sounds of goats talking amongst themselves. Jack looked from behind a bush. There was a clearing, with about ten goats in it.

Behind them, Big Rock was tied up securely with lots and lots of rope. And next to him was another troll, just as tied up.

They circled through the trees and bushes of the clearing until they reached Big Rock.

'Jack!' said Big Rock, his face lighting up into a big grin.

'Ssssh!' said Jack sharply. 'We don't want to alert the goats that we're here!'

Big Rock turned to the other troll. 'This Jack,' he said. 'I told you my friends would come and save us.' To Jack he said, 'This Taco Twister. He hates broccoli.'

Taco Twister nodded. 'Oh, if only I had a taco, I could get out of here!'

'I'll bear that in mind,' said Jack. He looked at the ropes that bound the two trolls. 'That's going to take a lot of untying,' he said. 'And I'm not sure if we've got the time.'

'You haven't,' said the phoenix.

The goats were shouting and charging towards them.

'Oh, for a taco!' groaned Taco Twister.

Jack turned to the phoenix. 'Can you burn those ropes?' he asked.

'Yes,' said the phoenix. 'But what about your friends?'

'You won't hurt us trolls; we're made of rock,' said Twister.

'Trolls like fire,' nodded Big Rock.

'And tacos. *Hot* tacos!' added Twister.

The phoenix let out a harsh breath . . . but instead of fire only a puff of smoke came out.

'Oh no!' groaned the phoenix. 'The change to a dragon and back must have used up my energy.'

'Try again!' urged Jack.

As the phoenix breathed out hard again the goats closed in on them, glowering.

This is bad, thought Jack, feeling desperate. *Maybe I will turn into Thud?* he hoped. Perhaps the terrible danger of this situation would be the switch that made him become the huge, raging troll, capable of hurling orcs and giants around.

But no. There was no feeling that came just before he turned into Thud, no shuddering, no glassy film over his eyes.

'Get them!' roared one of the goats. Jack found himself knocked down and trampled on by hooves. He looked up to see one goat standing over him, a gloating smile on its face as it lifted a hoof to crash down on him. But then the goat vanished, crashed aside, and instead Jack found himself looking into the face of Robin.

'To the rescue!' cried Robin triumphantly.

Now Jack saw that Milo, Princess Ava (in her Masked Avenger wrestling outfit) and Meenu were also there, all grappling with the goats and throwing them to the ground.

The goats, taken by surprise, began to fall back. But Jack saw two goats turn and aim their backsides at the intruders.

'Watch out!' yelled Jack. 'Farting goats!'

The two goats let off their noxious gases but, as they did so, the phoenix made another desperate attempt to breathe fire, and this time his hot breath ignited . . . and suddenly the gas from the goats exploded into flame.

BOOM!

The ball of flame enveloped Big Rock and Taco Twister and, as the smoke cloud cleared, Jack saw the two trolls lurch to their feet and flex their muscles and the ropes, already blackened and partly burnt through, snapped and fell away.

Immediately, Big Rock and Taco Twister waded into the battle.

Jack turned, looking for Milo and the others, and was shocked to see that four goats had got hold of Meenu in their powerful jaws and were pulling her in four different directions.

Milo, Robin and Ava, the Masked Avenger, were overwhelmed by the sheer number of goats that had come to the attack; and Big Rock and Taco Twister were also under siege as yet more goats appeared from different hiding places.

As Jack watched Meenu struggle and cry out, a sense of fury filled him at the unfairness and the cruelty of what the goats were doing. They had been horrible bullies the whole time. He strode towards the four goats and reached out, grabbed one, lifted it up . . . and kept lifting it.

Suddenly he realised that he had become *very* tall, and as he lifted the frightened goat up and threw it high into a nearby tree, he had become *very* strong.

'GRAAARRRRR!!!!'

The other goats holding Meenu looked up at him, and their mouths opened in shock and horror, releasing her to fall to the ground.

'Thank you, Thud!' she said as she got to her feet.

The giant troll, Thud, growled and reached

out to grab the other goats, but the goats had turned and fled, running off as fast as their hooves would carry them. The rest of the goats also decided to abandon the attack at the sudden appearance of this huge troll in their midst.

Within minutes, the Deep Dark Woods were clear of goats.

'You look strong,' said Milo, feeling the rock arm muscles of the Taco Twister.

'It's the tacos that do it,' replied the Taco Twister.

'Taco Twister join us!' declared Big Rock.

'Yes!' Ava grinned. 'We're going to fight Lord Veto and his horrible orcs.'

'I'll . . . I'll pay you in tacos,' said Milo, cunningly.

'Then, Lord Veto will feel the power of my tacos!' shouted the Taco Twister, and everyone cheered.

'Looks like we've got another member of our team,' said Ava.

'I think we have two,' said Jack quietly, stepping to stand next to the phoenix. 'We couldn't have escaped without you.'

Blaze shed a single tear. 'I will join you in your Quest, protect you and never leave your side, young Jack.'

There was a beating of wings, and the phoenix flew up and landed on the roof of the caravan, looking out for any danger that might come their way.

Milo climbed up into the driver's seat of the caravan, took out his map and said, 'Where to next?'

Chapter Four

As Big Rock and the Taco Twister circled their opponents in the ring, the chants for them rang out: 'Taco Twister in a spin. Have some Tacos; you will win!'

And:

'Big Rock, Big Rock, give us a pin. You're so strong; you're bound to win!'

Their opponents, two big local wrestlers called Lightning Rawr and Mr Belly, stood back-to-back in the centre of the ring, smug smirks on their faces, arms outstretched, waiting. This was a Devil Duo Match – two pairs of wrestlers in the ring at the same time. So far there had been one pinfall to each side. One more fall to decide the winner.

Mr Belly lived up to his name. He had a huge belly poking out in front, although the most noticeable thing about him was his enormously long moustache, the ends of which curled onto the ground.

'I don't get why they're smiling,' whispered Jack to Milo. 'They don't look at all worried.'

Suddenly, Rawr pointed a finger towards the Taco Twister and a burst of lightning flashed out from his finger and hit the big troll, burning a hole in his costume.

At the same time, Mr Belly swung the long

ends of his moustache like a lasso, wrapping them around Big Rock, tying his arms to his sides.

It was a tactic that would have worked on any other wrestler, but not on two large trolls made of rock.

Big Rock spun round and round, unwinding the ends of Mr Belly's moustache. Then he grabbed the ends of the moustache and swung them, and Mr Belly, high into the air.

Rawr's mouth dropped open in astonishment as he looked up at his wrestling partner, sent flying high above the ring. Suddenly the heavy figure of Mr Belly crashed down, right on top of Rawr.

'One,' counted the referee, 'two, three . . .'

The crowd went wild, and as the referee called out 'Ten!' they began their chants again:

'Trolls, trolls, here they come! Trolls, trolls, yay they've won!'

Rawr and Mr Belly struggled to their feet in the centre of the ring and glared at the two trolls.

'You haven't heard the last of us,' raged Mr Belly.

'We'll get you for this!' snarled Rawr. And he let off another flash of lightning from his fingers, but Big Rock just held up his big hand and the lightning bounced off it, back towards Rawr, and hit the canvas by his and Mr Belly's feet.

Rawr and Mr Belly gave a last scowl, and then marched up the aisle towards the exit, while Big Rock and Taco Twister climbed out of the ring.

'Great stuff!' Milo congratulated them.

'What do you think of that pair as wrestlers?' asked Taco.

Big Rock made a fart noise.

'Right,' nodded Milo in firm agreement. 'Not for *our* team!'

'Ava's next,' said Jack.

Princess Ava, in her cloak and costume and full head-mask as the Masked Avenger, was already in the ring, parading around as the audience cheered.

'Oh Princess Ava, do us a favour. Show those

baddies who is braver!' shouted the crowd.

'The next contest,' called the referee, 'is between the Masked Avenger, and our very own . . . Spiderella!'

'Spiderella,' scoffed Milo. 'What sort of name is that?'

'A woman wrestler with spiders?' suggested Jack. And he pointed. 'Look.'

Milo, Meenu and the two trolls followed Jack's gaze, and saw a young woman in a black costume slide under the ropes and get to her feet in the ring. As she did they realised that spiders were falling from her costume to the ring, running around her feet, and then climbing up onto her again.

'Wow!' breathed Milo, awed.

'How does she train those spiders to do that?' wondered Jack.

'Spiders not good for Ava,' muttered Big Rock, worried.

'I wonder how they'd taste in a taco?' asked Taco Twister.

'It's not a fair contest,' said Jack. 'It's Ava against another wrestler and loads of spiders. You ought to make an objection to the referee, Milo.'

'Maybe she'll leave the spiders in her corner when the match starts,' said Milo hopefully.

They never found out. There was a shout of, 'Stop this!' from the back of the hall, and the next moment a whole army of soldiers armed with spears and bows and arrows had crashed into the hall and marched down the aisles to the ring. A tall man with lots of medals on his uniform pulled himself up into the ring and addressed the referee, and the crowd.

'I am Major Mustard and, by order of King Nugget, this wrestling tournament is cancelled!

And the wrestlers are to be arrested and thrown in jail.'

'What!' shouted Milo, angry. 'On what charge?'

'Being rebels,' said Major Mustard. 'Take them away!'

Milo, Meenu and Princess Ava sat in a large cage inside a gloomy prison cell, while Big Rock and Taco Twister did their best to try and bend the bars of the cage open.

'It was lucky Jack managed to get away,' said Meenu.

'Yes. He'll get us out of this, I'm sure,' said Milo. He looked towards Big Rock. 'Any luck with those bars, Big Rock?'

Big Rock gave an unhappy sigh. 'No, they really strong.'

Taco Twister kicked the bars, but they didn't bend at all, even with his troll kick. He stamped his foot hard with frustration.

'Be careful where you're putting your feet,' said a little voice.

They all looked down, and saw that a teeny, tiny green frog had jumped, really fast, through the bars to join them in the cage.

'Hello, little frog,' said Ava. 'What are you doing here?'

'I'm here with a message from Jack,' said the frog. And the next second the frog had turned into Blaze, the phoenix.

'I can't get over how you do that!' exclaimed Meenu. 'That is so cool!'

'And useful,' said Blaze. 'This place is difficult to get into. I could only do it as a frog.'

'What's the message from Jack?' asked Milo.

'He wants you to know he and Robin are trying to get help. He promises he'll get you

out of this.' Then he changed back into the tiny frog. 'And I'm off to help them.' And with that, the frog hopped out through the bars of the cage and disappeared.

'I still don't understand why we got arrested,' grumbled Milo.

'Because you beat us,' said a nasty voice.

The gang turned, and saw that Lightning Rawr and Mr Belly had entered the cell and were smirking at them through the bars of the cage.

'You see, we're the sons of King Nugget, and we expect to win when we wrestle,' smiled Rawr. 'If we don't, then anyone who beats us is obviously disloyal to the King.'

'So that makes you rebels,' added Mr Belly.

'And rebels get locked up here for a very long time,' said Rawr.

'A *very* long time,' nodded Mr Belly. 'You're going to be inside this cage for years and years and years.'

'So long!' laughed Rawr. And he let fly with a burst of lightning from his fingertips that just missed Meenu. Then the pair left, slamming the heavy cell door behind them.

'Years and years!' Princess Ava gasped, horrified.

'We haven't got years and years,' burst out Milo. 'We've got a Giant Rumble to get to and win in ten days, or else we're out of business!'

'Jack will get us out,' said Big Rock confidently.

'I hope so,' said Taco Twister. 'I don't reckon they give prisoners tacos in here.'

Jack hated watching the soldiers take away his friends, but he knew he had to escape if he was going to save them. He snuck out of the wrestling ring with Robin the horse behind a group of Mr Belly supporters, all trailing pretend moustaches behind them.

'If we can't watch wrestling in the ring,' said one of the kids, who had stuffed a big pillow down his shirt to create a bigger belly, 'then let's go to the fair and see that Bendy Wendy!'

His friends all cheered, and Jack decided to follow them. 'We can hide in the crowd at the fair,' he whispered to Robin.

'As long as no one makes me give pony rides,' muttered the horse.

At the edge of town, the fair was busy. There were stalls with different sorts of games, and tents with fortune tellers and sideshow performers. Outside one large red-and-white striped tent was a board with a picture of a girl with very long arms and the words: BENDY WENDY. *You'll be amazed at what she can do!*

Jack realised that Bendy Wendy, with her long arms, might be just the person to help.

He nudged Robin. 'Maybe she can help us?'

Robin whinnied. 'Maybe she could, but why would she?'

Inside the tent, Jack took his seat on straw bales, along with the rest of the small audience. Robin and Blaze joined him. They had only just sat down, when there was a blast of music from the loudspeakers, and a tall, thin girl appeared, dressed in a bright pink leotard with the letter W on the front. What was amazing about her was her arms; they weren't just long – they were . . . long, long, long, long, long and completely bendy, like two very long, thin hosepipes with her hands at the end.

They watched as she did her act: first twisting her long arms together, then untwisting them and forming all sorts of shapes with them – houses; then animals, including the shape of a horse and a large bird which seemed to fly up into the air and then vanish as she unwound her arms.

Finally she made two characters with her arms, and added some voices. She did a little skit where an evil king chased a little girl, laughing horribly, then had her thrown in jail. But the little girl squeezed through the bars and escaped.

Amazed by her act, at the end Jack clapped his hands, while Robin banged his front hooves together and Blaze beat his wings and set off puffs of fire and smoke.

'I know she'll help us,' declared Jack. 'That skit at the end – I bet that king was supposed to be King Nugget.'

The trio followed Bendy Wendy as she left the stage and found her in a small room at the back of the tent.

'Hello,' said Jack. 'I'm Jack.'

'Nice to meet you,' said Bendy Wendy, smiling. 'Do you want my autograph?'

'Uh, yes,' said Jack, fumbling for a piece of paper.

'But really,' interrupted Robin, 'we want your help.'

Jack quickly told Bendy Wendy what had happened at the wrestling tournament.

Bendy Wendy's nice smile turned to a frown. She looked at her long arms and said, 'It was the King's two sons who made me like this, and I've vowed vengeance ever since.'

'Rawr and Mr Belly did this to you?' said Robin.

'They were as horrible when they were children as they are now. One day, for a joke, they grabbed me and pulled my arms, and kept pulling and pulling. Luckily for me, I had the kind of bones that don't break, but I ended up like this, with my arms stretched. When the King found out, instead of telling his sons off, he tried to have me locked up. But I managed to get away. I've spent the last few years living beyond the mountains, perfecting how to use these long arms of mine so I could come back and get rid of King Nugget and his two dreadful sons. And now that's what I'm going to do!'

'Oh no you're not!' came a shout.

They turned and were shocked to see Major

Mustard burst into the small room, with lots of armed soldiers.

'You have just admitted treason,' shouted Major Mustard. 'You are all under arrest! Soldiers, seize them!'

Chapter Five

Milo paced around the cage.

'Can you stop doing that?' asked Princess Ava. 'You're making me jumpy.'

'It's because he's frightened that we're never going to get out,' said Meenu.

'No it's not!' said Milo. 'Jack and Robin and Blaze will come up with a plan to get us out of here. In fact, it wouldn't surprise me if any moment now that door opens and Jack comes in and – '

At that moment, the cell door did open and Jack stumbled in, followed by a young woman with incredibly long arms and Robin the horse.

'Sorry,' said Jack apologetically. 'We got caught. Although Blaze got away.'

'Get in!' snapped Major Mustard, shoving them all inside the cage and clanging the door shut. 'And be quiet!' he commanded as he left the room.

'This is Bendy Wendy,' Jack whispered, to introduce the young woman.

'Great arms,' said Big Rock, impressed.

'Thank you,' said Bendy Wendy, stretching them out.

'Do you have any food?' asked Taco Twister hopefully. 'Something hot and spicy?'

'Sorry,' said Jack.

'He told you to be quiet,' sneered a new voice. Spiderella, still wearing her costume from the wrestling tournament, burst in the door. Her spiders ran up and down and in and out of her hair. She glared at Princess Ava – still wearing her Masked Avenger costume – through the bars.

'If we'd wrestled,' said Spiderella, 'I'd have beaten you easily.'

'Let me out of this cage and we can settle it now,' challenged Ava.

Spiderella gave a mocking laugh. 'Let you out of the cage? What sort of idiot do you think I am?'

'A spidery one,' snapped back Ava.

Spiderella shook her head. 'One day we'll wrestle and, when we do, I shall beat you! But right now, you can entertain my little friends.'

She made a low whistling sound, and the spiders scuttled across the floor towards the gang. They climbed up Big Rock first, biting him all over. Then they scattered and began to climb up everyone else.

'Help!' yelled Milo, trying to slap them off. 'This isn't fair!'

Spiderella laughed as her spiders attacked the gang. She didn't see the tiny frog hop past her and through the bars into the cage. He opened up his tiny mouth and an enormous

tongue snapped out and grabbed two spiders at once.

'Blaze!' said Jack. 'Is that you?'

The frog gobbled up two more spiders and Spiderella shrieked.

The spiders dashed back to their creepy mistress. 'You harmed my spiders,' she raged at them. 'I'll have my revenge for that!'

She stormed out of the cell. Inside the cage, the tiny frog turned into Blaze, the phoenix.

'Thanks, Blaze,' said Meenu gratefully. 'I thought those spiders were going to eat us alive.'

'Bites hurt,' said Big Rock, frowning.

'That was horrible,' said Milo. 'I don't like spiders!'

'Really? I love 'em!' said Taco, munching on a mouthful of spiders. 'Great peppery taste. They'd be fantastic in a taco.'

'Yuk!' said Milo.

'Much too much commotion down here for my liking,' declared Major Mustard, as he marched in and banged a cane against the bars of the cage. Behind him followed a short man dressed in royal robes and wearing a big golden crown.

'Stand to attention for His Royal Highness, King Nugget!' boomed Major Mustard.

Immediately, Milo rushed to the bars of the cage and appealed to the short man. 'We're not rebels, Your Majesty. We promise if you let us go, we will leave your country and never come back. We've got a very important wrestling tournament we must get to!'

'Really?' said a silky, evil voice, and they turned, shocked. Their old enemy, Lord Veto, slid into the prison. He chuckled. 'That is the point, you idiot. King Nugget is an old friend of mine, and when I heard you were going to his kingdom to find more Wrestling Trolls for your pathetic troop, I asked him if he would lock you up until after the Giant Rumble. When you and your so-called Wrestling Trolls don't turn up, victory will be mine. And that will be the end of you! Remember our agreement, Milo: the loser quits wrestling forever.'

'But this is a cheat!' protested Jack.

'We never said that we'd be fighting fair.' Lord Veto smiled like a snake. He bowed to King Nugget. 'Thank you for your help, Your Majesty, in keeping these dangerous rebels safely under lock and key.'

'Have you seen the coverage I've gotten because of this?' King Nugget said, shaking a newspaper at them and grinning. The headline read NUGGET NABS TERRIBLE TROLLS! 'And this one?' THE LEGENDARY MASKED AVENGER IS TAKEN CAPTIVE! 'It's fantastic! There has even been a news report by Melissa Hart and John Brown on News Flash Television,' he boasted. 'The only one who didn't cover us was the *Daily Wrestle*. How long do you want them kept locked up, my dear friend?'

'I think a month will do,' smiled Lord Veto. 'That will see the end of Waldo's Wrestling Trolls.'

With that, Lord Veto and King Nugget strode out, and the door of the cell clanged shut behind them.

'This is so unfair!' shouted Meenu.

'If I could just get my hands on that man.' Princess Ava scowled.

Milo looked at Jack. 'That was so unfair! It must have made you really angry,' he said, hopefully. 'Angry enough to turn into Thud?'

Jack shook his head and sighed. 'I'm afraid not.'

'We have to find a way to get out of here,' said Princess Ava.

'I've got an idea,' said Bendy Wendy. And then she began to shout, 'Help! Help! The prisoners are escaping!'

The others stared at her.

'What are you doing?' demanded Princess Ava.

Wendy ignored her and kept shouting, 'Help! Help!'

The door of the cell was unlocked and in burst Lightning Rawr and Mr Belly.

'What's all this shouting?' demanded Mr Belly angrily.

'If you don't shut up,' shouted Rawr, 'I'll send a burst of lightning in there and fry the lot of you!'

And then suddenly the expression on his face changed from a scowl to a silly smile, and then he began to laugh.

Mr Belly turned to him, puzzled.

'What's so funny?' he demanded.

And then, he too began to laugh.

It was then that the others saw that Bendy Wendy had slid her extraordinarily long arms through the bars and right up to Mr Belly and Lightning Rawr, and was tickling them under the arms.

'Stop!' begged Lightning Rawr, and he raised his hands to try and fire off a lightning bolt, but he was laughing so much he couldn't do it. Soon he and Mr Belly were lying on the ground, rolling about laughing, and the ring of keys fell onto the floor.

There was a flash as Blaze suddenly changed from a phoenix to a tortoise with a thunder-strike symbol on its back. While Bendy Wendy kept Lightning Rawr and Mr Belly helpless by tickling them, the daredevil tortoise nipped through the bars of the cell, picked up the keys and brought them back.

Milo unlocked the cage and the gang spilled out. They grabbed Mr Belly and Lightning Rawr and threw them into the cage, locking the door.

'There!' snapped Princess Ava. 'See how you like being locked up.'

As the two cheating wrestlers shouted their protest, the team crept out of the cell and stood in the corridor outside, listening.

'That's some move,' Milo said admiringly to Bendy Wendy. 'Have you ever considered wrestling?'

'Sshh!' said Meenu, as Wendy looked thoughtful.

'Okay,' said Jack, who had been quickly scanning the corridor, 'I think we're in luck. There aren't any soldiers around.'

But at that moment, out from the shadows leapt Major Mustard, holding a spear. 'I thought you'd try something like this.'

Immediately, the corridor was filled with soldiers, some armed with spears, some with swords, and all with shields as they leapt at the gang.

The two trolls, Big Rock and Taco Twister, grabbed the nearest soldiers and threw them at others. Robin did his best, kicking out with his hooves.

The Masked Avenger and Meenu worked as a tag team, tripping the soldiers to knock them over. Milo was impressed to see Bendy Wendy using her long arms as ropes, catching soldiers and banging their heads together, knocking them out.

'Tell me, Wendy,' said Milo, dodging a soldier who had been tossed in the air by Taco Twister. 'Do you like to travel?'

'More soldiers coming!' warned Big Rock, and they saw that at least twenty more soldiers were pouring into the attack.

'Yes, I do,' said Bendy Wendy as she tickled another soldier until he dropped his weapon.

'We're outnumbered!' wailed Robin.

'Do big crowds scare you?' Milo asked, stomping on a soldier's foot.

'No – I've been performing at the fair for ages now,' replied Wendy. 'But what does that have to do with getting us out of here?'

'This time, I'll make certain you'll never escape!' shouted Major Mustard.

'GRAAARRRR!'

The huge roar filled the narrow corridor, deafening everyone.

'I wish he wouldn't make that noise,' complained Robin. 'It hurts my ears.'

Where Jack had stood, now there was the massive figure of Thud the Troll, roaring loudly and grabbing up soldiers and hurling them aside as if they were made of paper.

'Wow!' said Bendy Wendy, awed. 'Who's that?'

'That's Jack,' said Milo.

Bendy Wendy looked bewildered.

'I'll explain later,' said Milo. 'Right now, I have another application question for you. How do you fancy joining Waldo's Wrestling Trolls?'

The caravan trundled along, pulled by Robin.

They'd left the Kingdom of King Nugget far behind them and were headed onwards.

'Looks like we've got one more for the team,' Jack said to Meenu and Princess Ava. They were sitting on the roof of the caravan while Big Rock and Taco Twister ran alongside, jumping and practising kicks. Milo was at the front, holding the reins and talking to Bendy Wendy.

'Bendy Wendy plus Big Rock, Taco Twister, the Masked Avenger and Thud,' Ava said, 'make five. We still need five more.'

'Has Bendy Wendy finished Milo's crazy application form?' asked Meenu.

The three shuffled forwards along the roof so they could get nearer to Milo and Bendy Wendy and listen as Milo ticked off her answers.

'Do you snore?' asked Milo.

'What a silly question,' snorted Bendy Wendy. 'What does that have to do with being a wrestler?'

'It's to find out if you'd keep everyone else awake when we're camping,' said Milo.

'I don't know,' said Wendy. 'I can't hear myself when I'm asleep. How many more of these questions are there?'

'Just a few,' he replied, pulling the caravan to a halt and jumping down.

'Do you like tacos?' called Taco Twister, and the others laughed.

'Yes!' said Wendy.

Milo pulled out a green scroll titled APPLICATION FORM. 'Do you agree to the terms and conditions?'

'I don't know what they are,' replied Bendy Wendy, sensibly.

Princess Ava jumped down from the roof and interrupted. 'Never mind all of Milo's silliness. The most important question is . . . can you keep a secret?' Princess Ava was still in her Masked Avenger costume. If they couldn't trust Bendy Wendy, they could never reveal Ava's secret identity.

Ava took a deep breath and took off her mask.

Wendy gasped. 'Yes, Your Royal Highness.' She bowed her head. 'I promise to always keep your secret.' She smiled. 'And I hope one day to wrestle with you!'

'Welcome,' declared Milo, 'to the newest member of Waldo's Wrestling Trolls!' And the whole team cheered. The whole team, except for one.

The cheering stopped as they heard a thud and looked to see Big Rock lying on the ground.

'He tripped over!' said Jack. 'I've never known Big Rock to do that before.'

Princess Ava had gone to the fallen Big Rock, and she looked worried.

'Don't feel good,' said Big Rock slowly.

'Oh no,' she said. 'He's ill.'

'Ill?' echoed Milo. 'Big Rock's never ill!'

Taco Twister had joined Ava beside the fallen Big Rock. 'The Princess is right. Look at those lumps where the spiders bit him.'

'Spiderella!' said Jack, realising.

'They must have had a special venom,' said Bendy Wendy. 'She'll never tell us how to cure him. There's no hope.'

'We have to find the cure!' cried out Jack. 'We have to!'

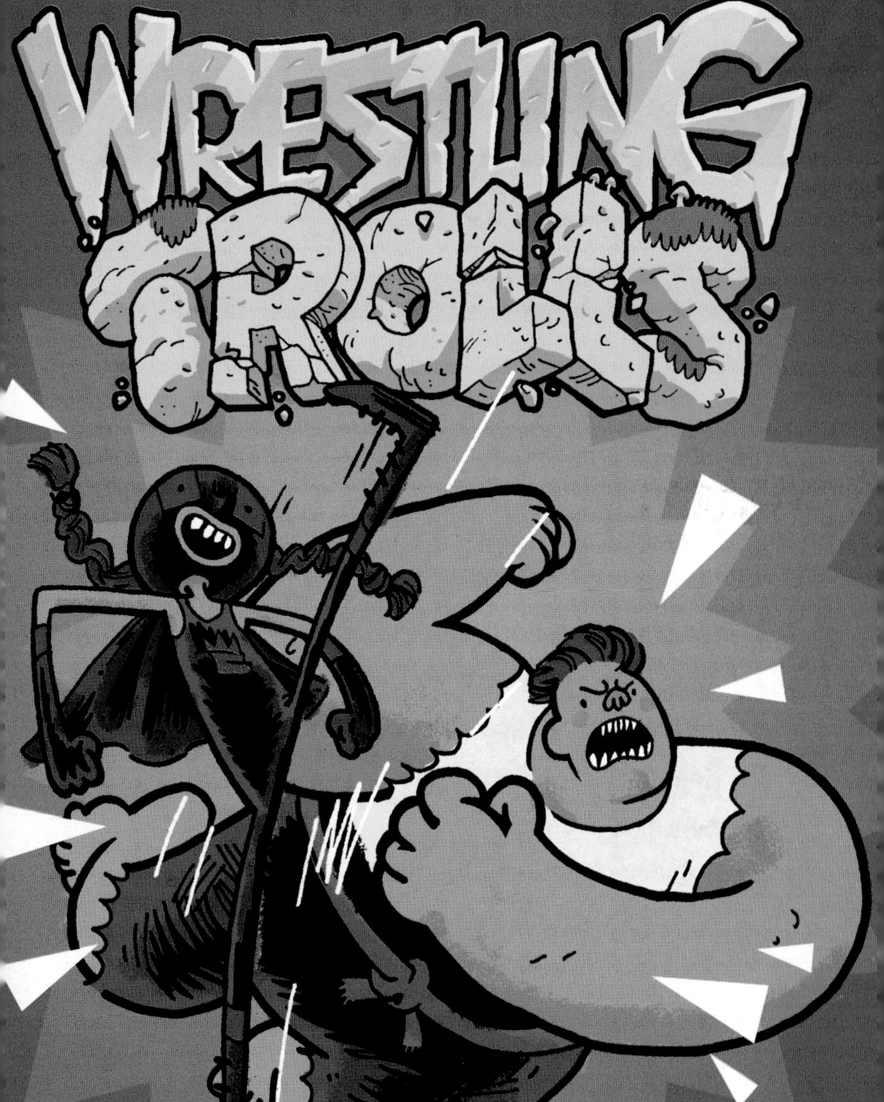

FUN & GAMES

Grab paper, pens, a friend
and complete the wrestling challenges!

SLOGAN SELECTOR

YOU WILL NEED:
A square sheet of paper, a pen and a friend.

TO MAKE

1. Fold each corner to the opposite corner. Open paper up. You should have creases in your paper that look like this.

2. Fold all corners into the centre of the paper like this.

3. Turn your paper over so the folds you just made are face-down.

4. Repeat step 2. Your paper should now look like this.

5. Label each of the top 4 quarters with one of Waldo's Wrestling Trolls: Jack, Princess Ava, Big Rock, Robin.

6. Label each of the 8 inside triangles with another wrestler's name. Choose one from the book or make up your own.

7. Underneath each flap write a wrestling chant – choose one from the list opposite or make up your own.

1

2

4

TO PLAY

1. Choose a wrestler from a top flap.
2. Spell out that character's name while opening and closing the selector in time with the letters.
3. Stop at the last letter and choose a wrestler from the four on show.
4. Repeat step 2.
5. Choose one more wrestler.
6. Open that flap and find your slogan.

SLOGANS

PRINCESS AVA, NO ONE BRAVER!

GET READY TO RUMBLE!   CRUSH HIM TO DUST!

SHOW THOSE BADDIES WHO IS BRAVER!

TWIST HIM LIKE A TACO!   PIN IT TO WIN IT!

CHOP HIM LIKE A PINE TREE!

TIME FOR BIG ROCK 'N' ROLL!

☐ I'VE DONE THIS!

DRAW A WRESTLING COMIC

Comics don't have to be funny; they can be any kind of story with pictures.

You can include speech bubbles or explanatory words, but try to keep words to a minimum.

We like to include fight sounds:

THUD!

BASH!

BIFF!

HOW TO DRAW A COMIC

STEP 1: Choose your characters.

STEP 2: Plan your story – something from this book, or make up your own!

Choose three to six specific moments from a scene. Then draw that number of boxes onto a piece of paper.

Each box will represent one moment of the story.

STEP 3: Draw!

TOP TIP!

It's a good idea to start in pencil, so you can erase, and then go over it in ink or colour once you're happy with how it looks.

I'VE DONE THIS!

DESIGN A SOUVENIR!

DESIGN A SOUVENIR WORTHY OF A TRIP TO SEE THE GIANT RUMBLE!

☐ **I'VE DONE THIS!**

Imagine you are at the stadium watching your favourite wrestler. What would you most like to buy from the merchandise stall as a souvenir? A trophy? A medal? A mug or a dinner plate?

MORE SOUVENIRS BY READERS:

A foam finger.

by Fancyfootball on
www.thestoryadventure.com

by Isapop on
www.thestoryadventure.com

TROLL CONSEQUENCES

HOW TO PLAY

Each player starts with a piece of paper and writes the first step of the story.

Fold the paper over the words so nobody can see them, then pass the paper to the player on the left.

Write the second step for the story below the fold, then fold and pass the paper on as before.

Continue until each of the steps have been written. Players take it in turns to read out the story to the others.

You will each need a pen or pencil and a piece of paper and at least one friend to play with.

1 - [choose a boy's name]
2 - met [choose a girl's name]
3 - at/on/in [choose a place]
4 - He said [say what he said]
5 - She said [say what she said]
6 - He did [say what he did]
7 - She did [say what she did]
8 - The consequence was [say what happened in the end]

☐ I'VE DONE THIS!

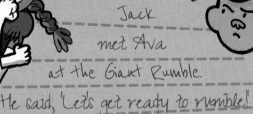

Jack
met Ava
at the Giant Rumble.
He said, 'Let's get ready to rumble!'
She said, 'I'm hungry for a taco.'
He did a backflip.
She got him in a collar tie.
The consequence was they both got tummy ache.

TACO TWISTER DINNER

I'VE DONE THIS! ☐

Design a meal
for the Taco Twister.
Make it as crazy as you
like to make sure this wrestler
has plenty of energy.

You can trace over this
dinner plate and draw
the meal.

WRESTLING RING

Had fun with these games and want more Wrestling Trolls action?

There's more fun and games waiting for you right now on **www.wrestlingtrolls.com** with challenges, activities to download and more facts about your favourite characters!

Join the Wrestling Ring and get a free finger puppet of Big Rock to battle with. Plus, upload your creations from this section and you can also earn yourself other exclusive treats.

Log on now to
www.wrestlingtrolls.com

Chapter Six

The whole group clustered round the fallen Big Rock, anxious.

'None of us were affected,' said Princess Ava. 'It must be a disease that only affects trolls.'

Robin looked at Taco Twister. 'You're a troll. Have you ever seen anything like this before?'

Taco Twister shook his head.

'How come you weren't taken ill?' asked Milo.

'None of the spiders bit me,' said Taco.

'Yes, but you ate them!' pointed out Jack.

'The Taco-Twister stomach can handle anything!'

Suddenly Meenu stiffened. 'Footsteps,' she whispered urgently. She pointed towards the edge of a large rockface. 'Someone's coming!'

'What if it's Major Mustard and his men?' asked Robin.

'Let me at them!' growled Princess Ava, and she ran to the edge of the rock.

'I'm with you, Princess!' said Taco, and they both dropped into a crouch. The rest of the team stood between them and Big Rock, who groaned quietly.

As the figures appeared round the edge of the rock, Ava and Taco sprang on them, wrestling them to the ground.

'Hey!' complained the smaller of the two, ducking out of Princess Ava's grasp. 'Is that how you welcome an old friend?'

'Grit!' exclaimed Jack joyously. He ran to the young troll wrestler and threw his arms around her in a hug. 'It's so great to see you!'

'When we didn't hear from you, we thought you hadn't got our message,' said Milo.

'I only got it a couple of days ago,' said Grit. 'I was at a Troll Wrestling Camp with –'

'Basil!' burst out Taco Twister delightedly.

He rushed over to the large troll who'd appeared round the rock with Grit, and the two bumped chests in a happy greeting.

The new arrival was a troll with flowers sprouting from the soil in all the tiny crevices in his rocky body and a ring of petals around his face.

'My old friend Basil!' yelled Taco. 'It's been too long since we've wrestled together.'

Meenu went to the new arrival and held out her hand. 'I'm Meenu,' she said, 'and I *love* your costume. All those flowers look lovely.'

'It just sort of grew on me,' smiled Basil.

Suddenly Grit saw the figure of Big Rock lying on the ground. 'What's happened?'

Bendy Wendy shook her head. 'He got bitten by spiders and . . .'

Basil hurried over to Big Rock, who had now turned green.

'It's called Rockoitus,' said Basil. 'If I'm right, in a few seconds his body will go back to its normal colour again . . .'

Even as Basil said the words, the green faded

from Big Rock and he was his usual colour once more.

'It's definitely Rockoitus,' said Basil. He shook his head. 'It's very rare. It only affects some trolls. But he's got it *very* bad. In about two minutes' time his tongue is going to start flashing yellow and black, and then he'll start sneezing spiderwebs. The worst thing is . . . eventually, he'll turn completely to stone.'

'Is there a cure?' asked Jack desperately.

'There is,' said Basil. 'But it's not easy to get hold of the ingredients.'

'What is the cure?' asked Milo.

'It's called Mediterranean Anti-Spider Tea. The ingredients are troll ale, six nine-year-old Mediterranean Brussels sprouts –'

'Wow, that stuff is lethal!' said Taco. 'It's so strong it can kill anything.'

'What else?' asked Jack urgently.

'Volcano dust, a cup of green slime, nine grey pebbles, and six pieces of coal. You stir all that together in a bowl, and give him a spoonful every five hours.'

'Then, team,' said Milo, standing up straight, 'you know what we have to do.'

Jack and Bendy Wendy walked into the small village. They'd found the nine grey pebbles they needed and the green slime, along with the pieces of coal, near where they were camped. But they still needed the other vital ingredients: the volcano dust, the troll ale, and the nine-year-old Mediterranean Brussels sprouts.

The gang had split up: Grit and Basil, with Robin, were staying with the unconscious Big

Rock to take care of him; Milo, Taco Twister, Princess Ava and Meenu had gone in one direction, while Jack, Bendy Wendy and Blaze had headed for the small village they'd seen from a distance.

'Where shall we start?' asked Bendy Wendy.

Jack pointed at a shop with a sign over it that said: CRUSHER'S CONVENIENCE STORE. WE SELL EVERYTHING.

Inside, the shop certainly did seem to have everything. It was the most crowded shop Jack

had ever seen. As Jack and Wendy stood there, looking at the different things stacked against the walls and even hanging from the ceiling, a deep voice said, 'I'm Crusher. Can I help you?'

They turned and saw that a huge man had appeared behind the counter and was looking at them suspiciously.

'We hope so,' said Jack.

Suddenly the man's expression changed and he pointed at Blaze. 'Is that a real phoenix?' he asked excitedly.

'Yes,' said Jack. 'Now, what we're looking for is . . .'

But before he could finish, the huge man had produced a large net and scooped Blaze up in it.

Immediately, Blaze burst into flames to burn his way out of the net, but the net didn't burn.

'Elf wire,' said Crusher. 'It doesn't burn.'

'Let my phoenix go!' shouted Jack angrily.

Crusher shook his head and gave an evil smile. 'Mine, now.'

'I think we've got a problem,' whispered Wendy to Jack.

Milo, Ava and Meenu followed Taco into a small café.

'I can't see how we're going to get ingredients here.' Milo frowned.

'It's worth asking,' said Taco.

'You've only chosen here because they sell tacos,' said Ava accusingly.

'Do they?' asked Taco Twister innocently. 'I hadn't noticed.'

'No?' snorted Meenu. 'You didn't notice that sign outside that said, *Great Tacos Here*?'

'Well, I *may* have done,' admitted Taco. But then his face lit up in a smile and he pointed at the menu chalked on the wall. 'But look there! Troll ale!'

'But no Mediterranean Brussels sprouts,' Ava pointed out.

'One thing at a time,' said Taco.

'Can I help you?' asked a voice, opening up a little door between the seating area and the kitchen. It was a man with spikey black hair, tattoos and a big black tongue. He was smiling,

but he didn't look
friendly.

'Yes, please,' said
Milo. 'We'd like
some troll ale, please.'

'And tacos!' added Taco Twister.

'Of course,' nodded the man, and gave that
sneaky smile again. 'But before I serve you,
you must answer my riddle.'

'Why?' asked Milo, puzzled.

'My name is the Incredible Pulk and, as the
best taco maker in the realm, only worthy
people are allowed to eat my tacos.'

'We haven't got time for riddles,' said Milo
impatiently.

'No time for riddles, no service,' said the
man, slamming the little door shut.

'No, wait!' said Milo, knocking on the door. 'We'll answer your riddle.'

The man peeped his head out of the door, his spikey earrings making him look even more menacing. 'What word spelled forwards means heavy, and backwards is not?'

Milo, Ava, Meenu and Taco exchanged bewildered looks.

'I have no idea!' said Milo.

'That is a pity,' sneered Pulk. 'In that case, there'll be nothing for you here!'

Jack and Bendy Wendy stood staring at Crusher as he held the blazing net with the burning phoenix inside it in his huge hands. 'Fire doesn't burn me.'

Jack moved towards Crusher, while Bendy Wendy flexed her enormously long arms, ready to snatch the wire net with Blaze inside from the big man's hands.

Crusher saw them move and shook his head. 'If you try anything, I'll crush this bird between my two hands,' he threatened. 'I am very strong.

That's why they call me Crusher.'

Wendy stepped back.

'That's better,' said Crusher. 'Now, what is it you wanted?'

'We want our phoenix back,' said Jack.

The big man laughed. 'No chance! But I'm fair. I'll swap it. What would you like?'

'Volcano dust. Troll ale. And nine-year-old Mediterranean Brussels sprouts,' said Jack.

'You'll find the volcano dust in a bin over there,' said Crusher, nodding towards a bin by the door. 'I don't sell beer. And the only place you'll find those particular Brussels sprouts is Lord Veto's garden.'

Lord Veto! thought Jack with alarm. Their most villainous enemy!

Jack and Bendy Wendy went to the bin and Jack began to fill a bag up with volcano dust.

'What are we going to do about Blaze?' whispered Wendy.

'Let's get the volcano dust, and then rescue him,' Jack whispered back.

* * *

'What word spelled forwards means heavy, and backwards is not?' groaned Milo. He shook his head. 'It's impossible!'

'Give up?' smiled the Incredible Pulk.

'No!' shouted Ava angrily.

'Any chance of a taco while we're working it out?' asked Taco Twister hopefully.

Pulk shook his head. 'No answer, no service.'

Taco groaned. 'I'm so hungry I could eat a ton of tacos.'

'That's it!' said Meenu. She turned to the Incredible Pulk and said triumphantly, 'The answer's a ton.'

Ava and Milo stared at Meenu in admiration.

'Of course!' shouted Ava. 'A ton is "not" backwards. Brilliant!'

Milo smiled at the Incredible Pulk, whose own sneaky smile had now vanished.

'Drat!' snarled Pulk.

Jack sealed the bag with the volcano dust inside it and turned to Crusher, still holding the wire net with Blaze inside. The phoenix's fire had gone out and he sat inside the net.

'I've always wanted a phoenix,' Crusher said. 'I love the way they burst into flames.'

'There's another great trick they do,' said Jack. 'One that's really useful.'

'Oh?' said Crusher. 'What's that?'

'Blaze!' called Jack. 'All change!'

And suddenly the phoenix changed into a fluffy rabbit.

Crusher stared at the rabbit in the net in horror, and threw it away from him. 'I can't stand rabbits!'

Immediately the rabbit changed again, this time into a big Labrador dog.

'But I love dogs!' uttered Crusher, and he reached out for it. But before he could grab hold of Blaze, Bendy Wendy had wrapped her long arms around his as if they were elastic.

'Run, Jack!' she called.

'Not without you!' he said, releasing Blaze from the net.

'No problem!' said Wendy, and she gave a sharp jerk of her arms, sending Crusher spinning around like a top before he crashed to the floor.

Jack and Bendy Wendy ran out of the shop, the Labrador bouncing along beside them. As they hit the road, Blaze turned back into a phoenix again, and then all three were heading back to where Big Rock was waiting.

They sat by the caravan and watched Basil mix the ingredients they'd brought back in a bowl. Big Rock still lay on the ground, unconscious, every now and then turning green and then back to his usual colour again.

'I think he's getting worse,' said Ava, worried. 'His tongue has been flashing yellow and black a lot more.'

'Will this cure work?' asked Milo.

Basil let out a sigh. 'Not without all the ingredients,' he said. 'We're still short of the sprouts.'

'And the only place they're found is in Lord Veto's garden,' said Taco.

'Then that's where we're going to go!' said Jack.

'But Lord Veto has an army of vicious Wrestling Orcs there to protect him,' said Basil. 'And they say there are dangerous creatures that roam the grounds.'

Jack nodded. 'They're right,' he said. 'I used to work for him as a kitchen boy. But I know my way around Veto Castle. And I'm going to get in there and get those sprouts!'

'And we're all coming with you,' said Milo. He looked at the unconscious figure of Big Rock on the ground, with his mouth open and his tongue turning yellow and black, and a spider's web forming around his nose. 'We're going to save our friend if it's the last thing we do!'

Chapter Seven

Jack stood on the roof of the caravan, looking towards Lord Veto's castle through the telescope.

'What can you see?' asked Bendy Wendy.

'Can you see the garden?' asked Milo.

'I can see the wall around it,' said Jack.

'I love gardens,' sighed Basil.

'You won't like this garden,' warned Jack, getting down from the caravan. 'It's got terrible things in it. Deadly things.'

'What sort of things?' asked Princess Ava.

Jack knelt down and began to draw with a stick in the dirt. He drew the outline of the garden's jagged walls. 'Here there are lots of human-trap plants,' said Jack, dropping pebbles into one corner of the dirt map. 'They're like those plants that eat flies – Venus flytraps – but these eat people.'

'So we stay away from them,' said Milo. 'We could go in from here.' He pointed to the other side of the map.

'On that side,' said Jack, 'I saw the Spider Plant, which draws people in with a web.'

'I bet Spiderella planted that,' scowled Princess Ava.

'Over here,' Jack pointed to the other corner, 'is a plant that looks so beautiful that everyone who sees it falls in love with it, are drawn right up to it, and when they get there – snap! Gobbled up!'

'Yuk!' said Taco.

'All along these walls are the Wait-a-whiles. Those are vines that burn and sting. Very painful.'

'There aren't any plants on these walls,' said Milo, pointing the area out with his own stick.

'It's not just the plants,' said Jack. He placed a row of pine cones where Milo was indicating.

'These are the statues around the garden. They look harmless, but they're really attacking machines, remote controlled by Lord Veto.'

Milo slumped back. 'Is there anywhere we can get in?'

Jack kept going. 'Here, it's a pond filled with piranhas, and over there are strange creatures that, when you look at them, become whatever is your worst nightmare. But the most dangerous of all is the Wrouse.'

'What's a Wrouse?' asked Taco. 'Is it hot and spicy?'

'It's a cross between a worm, a rat and a mouse. It's six metres long with a bodtail – a cross between a body and a tail. At first when you see it, it looks like a friendly, fluffy animal, all curled up. But once it uncurls, it's a killing machine.'

'How do you know all this?' asked Meenu.

'I told you – I used to work as a kitchen boy in Lord Veto's castle,' replied Jack.

'What about the Brussels sprouts?' asked Robin. 'Where are they? We've got to get some to save Big Rock!'

'I couldn't see them through the telescope,' Jack said. 'And I never went in the gardens when I worked there, but I remember hearing that they're in a greenhouse in the middle of the garden. To get to it, you have to find your way through a labyrinth, a maze. And if you get inside the greenhouse, the sprouts are protected by plants that give off a deadly gas. If you try and pull the sprouts off the plant, the sprout plants scream – just like a person – and the gas plants send out their deadly gas.'

'Wow!' said Taco, awed. 'This is some deadly garden!'

'But we have to do it,' said Milo. He pointed at the unconscious Big Rock, who was still turning different colours. 'Without those sprouts, Big Rock will get weaker and weaker, and may never wrestle again.'

Princess Ava gasped.

'I've been watching him,' added Basil gravely. 'He's getting worse.'

'Okay,' said Milo, taking charge. 'Let's not waste any more time talking about deadly plants and dangerous statues and killer Wrouses! Let's get in there and get those sprouts!'

Milo, Jack, Taco, Princess Ava, Grit, Bendy Wendy and Basil stood outside the stone wall that surrounded Lord Veto's garden. Blaze the phoenix had flown over the wall and was circling the garden, checking out the dangers. Robin and Meenu had stayed at the caravan, watching over the unconscious Big Rock.

'I've got an idea,' said Basil. 'All these defences will be on the lookout for intruders, so we could fool them if we disguise ourselves as plants.' He gestured at his own body, with flowers and weeds growing out of the crevices in his rocky skin, and the petals growing around his head. 'Like me.'

'That's clever,' nodded Taco. 'Does anyone know what a taco plant looks like?'

The gang were covering themselves with earth and foliage and flowers, when there was a flapping of wings and Blaze appeared.

'Well?' asked Milo.

'There's one thing Jack didn't mention,' said Blaze. 'There's a whole army of gnomes in there, guarding the garden.'

Jack took a deep breath. 'How many?' he asked, not sure if he wanted to know the answer.

'It looks like hundreds – tiny people with different coloured hats and clothes. And there's a troll gardener there. He looks old, but he looks mean.' Blaze turned to Basil. 'He looks a lot like you: flowers growing out of his head, plants growing out of his body, but all his plants look dead and withered.'

Basil looked at the phoenix, shocked. 'It can't be!'

'It can't be what?' asked Princess Ava.

'I have a twin brother, another Wrestling Troll. His name is Green-Taker, because, like me, he loved plants. But then . . . we had an argument.'

'What about?' asked Jack.

'About the way we wrestled. He said we should be sneakier; I said wrestlers should be fair and honest.' Basil sighed. 'The trouble was, he'd met Lord Veto, who poisoned his mind and brainwashed him. One day he disappeared and I haven't seen him since.'

'I'm sorry, Basil,' said Princess Ava sympathetically.

Basil gave an unhappy sigh again. 'It was Green-Taker's decision,' he said. 'If it *is* him working in that garden, and I have to wrestle him to get to those Brussels sprouts, so be it.'

To get over the wall, the three trolls – Taco, Grit and Basil – formed a troll ladder, standing one on top of the other, and Bendy Wendy, Milo, Jack and Princess Ava climbed up them to the top of the wall.

Once there, Bendy Wendy let down her enormously long, rope-like arms and

grabbed the
trolls one at a
time, hauling
them up to the
top of the wall.
Then they all
dropped down
into the garden.

'There are the
statues!'
whispered Jack.
They looked at
the large grey
sculptures on
their pedestals.
Each one had a
weapon of some
kind: swords,
bows and
arrows, a scary-
looking spiky
chain and even a
three-pronged

fork – a trident.

'Move slowly,' hissed Basil. 'They'll think we're just plants, blowing in the wind.'

They crept along, past the statues. Although the eyes of the statues moved, the figures themselves remained fixed, their weapons frozen in stone.

Just as they got past the statues, Jack's arm brushed a little bush with no leaves.

Pop! Pop!

Two little twigs exploded.

'Ssshhh!' demanded Princess Ava and Jack stepped away from the exploding twigs.

'Sorry,' he whispered back. Stealing a quick glance at the statues, he was relieved to see that they didn't seem to have noticed the sounds.

Past the exploding twig bushes was a wobbly bridge over a large pond into which a waterfall poured.

'That bridge doesn't look like it will take the weight of a troll,' muttered Grit.

'No problem,' said Taco. 'We can wade through the water.'

With that, he plunged into the pond, and as he did so they saw the water come alive with thrashing fish, which leapt out and began to attack Taco with their sharp teeth.

'Piranhas!' exclaimed Milo.

Taco pushed his head above the surface of the water and laughed.

'They can't hurt us!' he laughed. 'We're trolls with rocky bodies!'

'I was thinking about us humans,' said Milo nervously. 'This bridge looks pretty wobbly, and if *we* fall into that pond . . .'

'Don't think about it!' urged Jack. 'Just run over it as fast as you can. And one at a time, otherwise it might break. You first, Wendy.'

Bendy Wendy nodded and darted across, but the others could see the wooden slats on the bridge starting to break up as she ran over them.

'You next, Princess,' said Milo.

Ava frowned and then took fifteen steps away from the bridge. She broke into a run, speeding towards it. As she reached the edge of the bridge she hurled herself into the air, somersaulted, and then landed on the other side.

'Wow!' said Jack. 'That was cool!' He turned to Milo. 'Do you think you can do that?'

'Never in a million years,' said Milo. He looked at the far side of the bridge, where Basil, Grit and Taco were clambering out of the water and joining Wendy and Princess Ava on the other side. Taco pulled a wriggling piranha off his arm, where it was trying to eat him, and pushed it into his mouth and began chewing.

'Hmm,' he nodded. 'Not as good as a taco, but not bad.'

'Here I come!' shouted Milo, and he began to run across the bridge. Even as he did so, the already broken slats of wood broke up further and tumbled into the water. Suddenly the wood around him began to crumble and he was about to tumble into the pond when Bendy Wendy's arms reached out and grabbed him, pulling him to safety.

Jack began his run, leaping from broken piece of wood to broken piece of wood but, halfway across, the bridge suddenly tipped and collapsed beneath him, and Jack crashed down, feeling the water close over his head.

Immediately the piranhas began to attack him, their sharp teeth tearing painfully at his arms and body, the savage, vicious killer fish pulling him down beneath the water as they tore at him. He was drowning and being eaten alive at the same time!

And then suddenly the sharp teeth of the

piranhas weren't hurting him any more. And he wasn't drowning. He was standing up with his head above the surface of the water – *well* above the surface of the water. He strode out of the pond, his heavy, rocky feet crashing on the ground.

'Hello, Thud,' grinned Milo, looking at the giant troll with relief.

Suddenly there was a cry of alarm from Princess Ava. 'Gnome alert!'

Hundreds of small garden gnomes had burst out through the bushes and were rushing towards them, waving small axes and spades and trowels.

'Time for trolls!' yelled Taco.

And he fell down and rolled himself towards the oncoming gnomes at speed. Grit and Basil realised what his plan was, as did Thud, the

giant troll that had once been Jack, and soon all four trolls were rolling over the army of garden gnomes, squishing them into the earth.

As the last garden gnome sank into the ground, the four trolls got to their feet. Or rather the three trolls – because Thud had already begun to shrink back to small Jack again.

'We've beaten the statues and the gnomes,' said Taco proudly.

'Yes, but how do we get back?' asked Princess Ava, looking at the shattered wood, floating on the surface of the piranha-filled pond.

'We'll cross that bridge when we come to it,' shrugged Milo.

'That's my point; there *isn't* a bridge,' said Princess Ava.

'No,' said Basil nervously. 'But I think that's a Wrouse!'

And they followed where he was pointing his finger and saw that a huge, long creature, part furry, part slimy, had slithered into view and was rearing up, ready to attack!

Chapter Eight

The Wrouse reared up higher, its vicious eyes fixed on them, and as its mouth opened they could see its sharp teeth, ready to tear at them.

'Look out!' yelled Jack.

They threw up their arms to try to protect themselves. Suddenly there was a blur as Blaze flew over their heads and straight into the Wrouse and turned into a multi-limbed octopus, which wrapped its legs around the hideous creature. The Wrouse crashed to the ground, with Blaze clinging to it. There was a blinding flash as the phoenix burst into flames, and the smell of burnt fur and skin came to their nostrils.

'Quick!' yelled Milo. 'Run!'

They ran, heading for the maze made of high

hedges that protected the greenhouse where the precious Brussels sprouts were growing.

'We're running out of time,' called Princess Ava. 'Only twenty minutes left to give Big Rock the sprouts, before he'll never wrestle again!'

'We can do it,' said Grit.

There was a flap of wings and Blaze appeared, back in phoenix shape.

'Thanks, Blaze,' said Taco. He smiled. 'But that smell of burning Wrouse . . . mmmmm! Makes me think of a hot taco!'

'Do you ever think of anything else but eating tacos?' demanded Bendy Wendy crossly.

'What else is there?' asked Taco. 'Tacos and wrestling! Fantastic!'

As they reached the entrance to the maze, a strange figure blocked the opening in the hedge. His face looked just like Basil, but the rest of him was very different.

Where beautifully coloured flowers grew from Basil's rocky troll body, this troll had dead and withered plants dropping from the earth in his body's cracks, and sharp-thorned

bramble
draped him
like a cloak.
And in his
hands he held
a large garden
spade.

'You're not
getting any
further!' he
grated
menacingly.

'Green-
Taker, is that
really you?'
asked Basil.

The bramble-draped troll peered
at the flowery troll. 'Basil?' he asked.

'Yes!' cried Basil. And he ran towards to the
troll, his arms outstretched in greeting.

'Watch out!' warned Grit as Green-Taker
swung his garden spade up. But as Basil threw
his arms around his long-lost twin brother in

a hug, Green-Taker threw the spade aside and threw his own arms around Basil.

'I wondered what had happened to you!' said Basil.

'It was Lord Veto,' said Green-Taker. 'He promised me everything if I came and worked for him: riches, luxury. He lied!'

'Yes,' said Jack grimly. 'That's Lord Veto for you.'

'This reunion is very touching,' said Princess Ava, 'but we are on a mission and time is running out! We need to get hold of the sprouts.'

'The Mediterranean Brussels sprouts?' asked Green-Taker.

'Yes,' said Jack. Quickly, they explained to Green-Taker about Big Rock being poisoned by Spiderella, and the final part of the antidote being the precious and rare sprouts.

'Will you help us?' asked Basil. 'We have to save our friend!'

'Yes,' nodded Green-Taker.

'Great! And then maybe you can join us in the Giant Rumble?' suggested Milo.

'There won't be a Giant Rumble if we don't save Big Rock!' snapped Princess Ava.

'How do we find our way through the maze?' asked Bendy Wendy.

'Follow me,' said Green-Taker.

As they entered the maze and followed the troll through the twisting and turning lanes of high green hedges, Green-Taker said, 'The maze isn't the problem.'

'Why?' asked Taco.

'Because once you've solved the maze, you'll come up against Vinesse and Whiff. They're the guardians of the greenhouse.'

'The poison plants!' said Jack.

'Yes,' nodded Green-Taker. 'The poison gas they give off is lethal.'

Basil smiled. 'To humans, maybe. But we're trolls. We don't have lungs that breathe air.'

'Yes, but Vinesse and Whiff have been working on a new poison gas that attacks rocks,' warned Green-Taker. 'It breaks them up. It will kill trolls.'

They came out of the maze of hedges and

there, in front of them, was the greenhouse. Inside, they could see the air was thick with some sort of purple smoke.

'Poison gas,' said Ava.

Basil had stopped smiling. 'Have Vinesse and Whiff perfected that troll-killer gas?' he asked, worried.

'I don't know,' admitted Green-Taker.

'Guess there's only one way to find out,' said Taco.

And then, before they could stop him, he had rushed to the greenhouse, pulled the doors open and plunged inside, disappearing in the clouds of purple smoke. The others stared, horrified. Just as Grit and Basil were about to rush in after him, they were stopped by a hideous screaming sound from inside the greenhouse.

'Oh no!' said Wendy, horrified. 'That's Taco!'

The next second the figure of Taco burst out of the greenhouse. In his hand he was holding a Brussels sprout plant.

'No,' he grinned. '*This* is Taco!' He held up the sprout plant, which was giving off the loud screaming sound, and winced. 'You didn't warn me they screamed so loud when you picked them!'

'Put those sprouts back!' shouted a muffled voice.

They turned and saw that two figures had come from round the corner of the greenhouse, a man and a woman. Both were wearing gas masks and holding gas canisters in their hands.

'Vinesse and Whiff!' exclaimed Green-Taker in horror.

Vinesse pointed her gas canister at them.

'One squirt of this and you will all die,' she snarled. 'Human and troll alike!'

'She means it,' said Green-Taker.

A shadow fell over the greenhouse, and they all looked up and saw that Blaze had turned into a huge green dragon and was descending, his mouth open wide.

WOOOSHHHH!

A burst of flame from Blaze hit Vinesse and Whiff and then . . . BOOM!! The gas canisters they'd been holding blew up in a cloud of thick black smoke and red fire.

When the cloud cleared, they saw the pair lying on the ground, smouldering.

'Blaze! You are the hero today!' said Jack.

'Quick! We don't have long left!' said Ava.

'Follow me!' shouted Green-Taker, and he led the way back through the maze, the others following, and Taco holding onto the precious Brussels sprout plant. By now it had stopped screaming.

They burst out of the maze and ran to the pond and the remains of the bridge.

'How are we going to get across?' asked Taco.

'Blaze,' said Jack, 'can you carry us over? You could fly us straight to Big Rock!'

Blaze huffed and puffed. 'I can't. Too tired. Done . . . too . . . much . . . changing.'

'Don't worry,' said Jack, stroking his friend. 'You've been such a big help already.'

'I can make a bridge,' said Wendy. 'If I stretch my arms across the pond, the lightest ones can climb over them.'

'Jack, that's you and me,' said Princess Ava.

'Taco, give me the plant.'

'Don't drop it in the pond!' warned Jack. 'The piranhas will gobble up the sprouts.'

'I won't,' said Ava determinedly. She stood poised as Wendy stretched her arms over the broken bridge. Just as Ava was about to make her way across this new makeshift bridge, they heard a hissing sound and saw the Wrouse coming at them again. Its fur and skin were singed and blackened, with smoke still coming from it, but there was no mistaking that the Wrouse was still alive, and still very dangerous.

'No!' yelled Green-Taker. He rushed forwards, grabbed hold of the Wrouse and threw the creature into the pond. Immediately, the water came alive as the piranhas leapt upon the singed creature.

'Go for it!' yelled Milo to Ava.

Ava began to clamber along the remains of the broken bridge, using Wendy's arms as rails in the places where there were gaps, all the time making sure the precious Brussels sprout plant was kept well away from the water. Just as she jumped off on the other side, a familiar and nasty voice spoke from behind them. 'Well, look what we have here!'

Lord Veto was smiling nastily at them. 'Fancy seeing you!' he sneered. 'So, you weren't scared off by my special weapon – Mr Belly and his brother.'

'Those two idiots!' said Milo scornfully. 'Is that the best you can throw at us, Veto?'

Lord Veto smiled. 'No,' he said. 'I have something much better!' Then he called out, 'Gnomes, to your master!'

With a shock, Jack and the others saw the ground around them begin to shake and heave, and the small garden gnomes they thought had been crushed appeared, bursting up out of the ground.

'Gnomes, attack!' shouted Lord Veto.

But instead of attacking, the gnomes just stood there, shaking, and Jack realised that they were actually laughing.

'Gnomes attack!' repeated Lord Veto, louder and angrier this time.

'Yes, Sir, we will,' nodded the leader of the gnomes. 'But . . .' and he began to laugh even harder, pointing at Lord Veto's bottom. 'You've got toilet paper stuck to your trousers!'

And all the gnomes began to laugh.

Lord Veto scowled and glared at the gang as he took the piece of toilet paper off his bottom.

'Silence!' he shouted at the gnomes.

The gnomes stopped laughing at once.

'You did this!' he hissed in menacing tones at the gang.

Taco Twister shrugged. 'Hey, I thought it was funny!' he said. 'I had this toilet roll on me and I thought –'

'You humiliated me in front of my gnomes,' roared Lord Veto. 'This will lead to some serious consequences in the wrestling ring!' And then he smiled again, an evil, nasty smile. 'Oh wait, you won't be there to fight, will you?' He raised his hands up. 'Gnome King! I summon you!'

All the little gnomes stopped giggling as the ground began to shake. Up from the middle of the miniature army rose an enormous, gnarled gnome, with hideously bad breath.

'Don't breathe in!' shouted Green-Taker. 'His breath will kill humans.'

'Get Jack and Milo out of here, Wendy!' shouted Taco Twister.

Lord Veto pointed a bony finger at them. 'Gnome King, capture them!'

Immediately, the army of gnomes and the Gnome King rushed at the gang.

'Quick!' shouted Bendy Wendy. 'Grab on!'

Jack and Milo clung to Wendy as she grabbed hold of the branch of a tree on the other side of the pond and pulled herself across, next to Princess Ava.

Wendy hit the ground and rolled, then bounced to her feet.

Milo, Jack, Ava and Blaze looked across to the far side of the pond, where the four trolls – Taco, Basil, Green-Taker and Grit – were disappearing under the weight of a mass of multicoloured garden gnomes.

'We've got to help them,' said Jack. The trolls had now completely disappeared beneath the army of gnomes.

'We haven't got time!' said Milo. 'We have to get the sprouts to Big Rock right now!'

As Milo, Bendy Wendy and Ava ran for the garden wall, Jack looked at the mass of moving gnomes. A second later the four trolls surfaced. Grit, Taco, Basil and Green-Taker had all been firmly tied up and lifted up on the backs of the gnomes.

'We'll come back for you!' yelled Jack. 'We'll

find you!'

'You won't find them,' cackled Lord Veto. 'And with no trolls for the Giant Rumble, that fool Milo's career in wrestling is over! Ha, ha, ha, ha, ha!!!' Then he turned to the army of gnomes and ordered, 'Take them to the Dungeon of Doom!'

Chapter Nine

Milo, Jack, Princess Ava, Bendy Wendy and Meenu sat on the steps of the caravan and watched Big Rock as he ran around. He jumped up into the air, did a series of punches and kicks and finished with a roll that landed him right in front of Princess Ava with a grin on his face.

'You seem to be fully recovered,' said Robin the old horse.

'All better now!' said the troll, giving Princess Ava a little hug. 'Thanks to you guys.'

'But we've still got a problem,' said Milo. 'Two, in fact. In just over an hour the Giant Rumble is supposed to start: ten of our wrestlers against ten of Lord Veto's. And four of our team, Taco Twister, Grit, Basil and Green-Taker, are locked up in Lord Veto's Dungeon of Doom. And if we don't turn up with a full team . . .'

'We'll be disqualified and lose,' said Meenu.

'It's more than just losing this Giant Rumble,' cried Milo. 'If we lose, I'll have to quit wrestling forever! It'll be all over! No more Waldo's Wrestling Trolls!'

'I said you were a fool to bet with Lord Veto,' snorted Robin. 'He cheats!'

'Arguing about it won't help,' said Princess Ava. 'We have to get the others out of this Dungeon of Doom.'

'The trouble is, we don't even know where it is,' sighed Bendy Wendy.

'You used to work for Lord Veto, Jack,' appealed Milo. 'You must have some idea where the Dungeon of Doom is.'

'I knew about some of the terrible things at Veto Castle, but I never heard of the Dungeon of Doom.'

'The Dungeon of Doom,' said Robin thoughtfully. 'It sounds *old*.'

'That doesn't help,' groaned Jack. 'The castle is old. The garden is old. Everything about Lord Veto's place is old!'

'Except for the new wrestling stadium,' pointed out Meenu. 'That's brand new. I hear it cost a million pounds to build!'

'Yes, but even that's built on somewhere that's old . . .' said Jack in frustration. Then he stopped and his mouth dropped open and his eyes grew very wide.

'What's happened to him?' asked Princess Ava.

'Is he turning into Thud?' asked Bendy Wendy, worried.

'No,' said Milo, shaking his head. 'He's just

remembered something very important.'

'Well I wish he'd share it with us,' grumbled Robin.

'The brand new stadium!' burst out Jack excitedly. 'It's built on the place where there used to be an old torture chamber and dungeon!'

'The Dungeon of Doom?' asked Ava.

'It has to be!' cried Jack.

'Are you sure?' asked Milo doubtfully. He looked at his watch. 'Time is running out, and if we spend a lot of time looking for this place under the stadium and you're wrong . . .'

'I'm sure I'm right!' said Jack.

'Okay,' nodded Milo. 'So, how do we get in?'

The dungeon was dark and smelly. It smelled of mould and sewage and dead rats and cheese. The only light came from glow-worms crawling over the walls.

In the gloom, Grit, Basil and Green-Taker watched as Taco Twister paced around, stopping every now and then to punch his fist against a wall.

'Punching the walls won't help,' said Basil.

'All you'll do is hurt yourself.'

'I'm thinking I can punch our way out of here,' growled Taco.

Grit shook her head. 'No chance,' she said. 'These walls look too thick.'

'She's right, they are,' said a new voice.

They turned to see where the voice had come from, and out of a gloomy corner stepped a garden gnome.

'Grrrr!' yelled Taco angrily, and he threw himself at the gnome. It was Lord Veto's gnomes that had tied them up and dumped them in this dungeon.

The gnome dodged to one side. 'Wait!' he appealed. 'I'm a prisoner in here, just like you!'

Taco stopped, puzzled. 'A prisoner?' he repeated.

The gnome nodded. 'My name's George, and I was made by Lord Veto, just like all the rest of the gnomes. But Lord Veto decided I was a Wrong Gnome, so he put me in here.'

'What's that mean?' asked Grit. 'A Wrong Gnome?'

'Well, all the other gnomes are . . . um, vicious and nasty. But I like pretty things. Especially flowers and butterflies and beautiful things in the garden.'

'That is so nice!' said Basil. He gestured at Green-Taker, his twin. 'My brother and I are Garden Trolls.'

'So, how do we get out of here?' said Taco.

'You don't,' sighed George. 'This place is underground. No one ever comes here.'

'Oh dear,' said Basil.

Black rats and cockroaches scuttled around and hid in the dark corners. Bats detached themselves from the ceiling and flew past the prisoners from wall to wall, while spiders of all kinds scuttled across the floor and up the walls.

'At least we're safe here,' said George.

'Safe?' echoed Grit.

'Yes,' said George. He pointed at a door in one wall. 'That's the only way out, and it leads to the torture chambers. Terrible things go on in there.'

'He's right,' said Green-Taker sadly. 'All the time I worked for Lord Veto, everyone was afraid of upsetting him, in case they were taken to the torture chambers. There's one that's a pit, and inside it is a Wrouse. But the worst one is the Laughing Room.'

'That doesn't sound so bad,' said Basil. 'Laughing is good.'

'Not in that room,' shuddered Green-Taker. 'The things in there make people laugh to death. There are tickling feathers, laughing gas, a book of terrible jokes and, the most fearful of all, a tickling machine which has loads of arms and hands with feathery gloves on.'

'Okay, so we don't go through that door,' said Grit.

Suddenly they were aware of the ghostly shape of a woman coming through the wall and floating towards them. She was dressed in rags, and her face was the most agonised they'd ever seen. She looked at them, gave a moan, and then floated upwards and disappeared through the ceiling.

'Who was that?' asked Basil, awed.

'That's one of the ghosts,' said George. 'This dungeon is guarded by the spirits of people who died here. If anyone tries to get out, they fly off and warn Lord Veto's guards.'

'So we really *are* trapped,' said Grit unhappily.

'Hey, it's not all bad!' exclaimed Taco.

They turned, and saw that he was examining what appeared to be a splodge of blood on the wall. He put his nose against it and sniffed. And then, to their shock, he stuck out his tongue and licked it.

'Yuk!' exclaimed Grit.

'Now that *is* gross!' said Green-Taker.

'No.' Taco smiled. 'It's ketchup. Great!'

Milo pulled Robin and the caravan to a halt in the caravan park by the brand-new wrestling stadium.

'We're here!' he called out. 'What next?'

'I don't know,' called back Jack. 'I have no idea how he built the stadium over the dungeon. Maybe we look for an underground entrance?'

Milo, Jack, Wendy, Ava and Meenu together with Big Rock, Robin and Blaze, looked at the huge new stadium. The whole building was lit up with coloured lights. All around it were huge ice sculptures.

'Great stadium!' said Big Rock in admiration.

There were long queues of people waiting to get in, many with placards and foam fingers.

Milo looked anxiously at his watch. 'Half an hour to go,' he said gloomily. 'We're never going to find them in time. We've lost!'

A sudden commotion of shouting made them

look. A door in the side of the building had been thrown open and a load of gnomes were throwing out a large troll, who was trying to fight them off. It was no use.

As the troll got to his feet, Lord Veto appeared in the doorway.

'If I ever see you here again, I shall have my gnomes put you in the Dungeon of Doom!' shouted Lord Veto. Then he spotted the gang standing there, and his face lit up in an evil smile. He strode over and leered at them.

'Well, well!' he said. 'Milo – and what remains

of his crew. So you made it to my stadium just in time for the Giant Rumble. What a pity you haven't got all your wrestlers with you! I wonder why that is?' And with that he threw back his head and laughed. Then he turned on his heel and stomped back inside the stadium, his gnomes following him, and slammed the door shut.

'I hate him!' growled Milo. 'He's a cheat.'

'Yes he is,' agreed the troll. 'I worked on building this stadium for him, and when I went to get my pay, he had his gnomes throw me out.'

'You helped build this?' asked Jack.

The troll nodded.

'My name's Bricks,' he said. 'I'm a troll builder, and also a wrestler. That's why I wanted to work on this place. It's a fantastic wrestling stadium! It's even got a revolving ring so that everyone in the audience can see what's happening. It's operated by orcs working cogs and pulleys and things.' He shook his head angrily. 'I was so looking forward to seeing tonight's opening event: the Giant Rumble!'

'We were looking forward to taking part in it,' sighed Princess Ava.

Bricks looked at them and frowned, puzzled. Then his face cleared.

'Wait! If you're Milo, then the rest of you must be Waldo's Wrestling Trolls.' He grinned at Big Rock. 'I certainly recognise Big Rock, the most famous Wrestling Troll of all. Wow! This is going to be fantastic! Have you seen who Lord Veto has got lined up against you?' And Bricks began to tick the names off excitedly on his fingers. 'Spiderella, Mr Belly, Lightning Rawr, Professor Broccoli, Hardcore, Princess Snuggle, Squarehead, the One-Eyed Gangster, Time-Master, and Footballio!' Then Bricks frowned as he looked at the small crew. 'So, where's the rest of your team?' he asked, looking around.

'In the Dungeon of Doom,' groaned Milo.

Bricks looked at him, shocked. 'What!' he said.

'As you helped build this place, do you know

where the Dungeon of Doom is, and how we get to it?' asked Jack.

'Yes,' said Bricks. 'It's in the middle of the stadium, right beneath the wrestling ring. But there's only one way in.' He shuddered. 'And that's to get thrown in as a prisoner. And if that happens, you'll never get out again, ever.'

'Maybe, maybe not,' said Jack thoughtfully. Then he smiled. 'But I have a plan!'

Chapter Ten

'There's no way out of this place,' said Green-Taker. 'We're trapped here forever.'

'Our friends will find a way,' Grit assured him confidently. 'Trust me.'

Suddenly, the door burst open and Big Rock crashed onto the dungeon floor, followed by Milo, Jack, Princess Ava, Bricks, Bendy Wendy, Meenu and Blaze. A big group of gnomes appeared, carrying Robin the old horse, and throwing him in as well.

'You can all stay here and rot!' shouted the Chief Gnome. With that, the door slammed.

Green-Taker sighed. 'I thought you said they were going to rescue us?'

'We are!' said Meenu as she got to her feet

and dusted herself off. 'This is Jack's plan.'

Taco stared at Jack. '*This* is your plan?' he echoed. 'To get locked up in the Dungeon of Doom, so there is no one outside to rescue us?'

'Yes, *I* didn't think much of it, either,' said Robin.

'Until Jack explained it to us,' said Princess Ava.

'And I *still* didn't think much of it,' snorted Robin.

'But it's the only plan we've got,' said Milo. 'It's only ten minutes before the Giant Rumble is due to start, and if we're not in that ring by then . . . we lose. And that means we have to quit wrestling forever.'

'If we don't get out of this dungeon, we're going to be *here* forever!' exploded Taco.

'What's your plan, Jack?' asked Grit.

Jack gestured at Bricks. 'This is Bricks, who worked on building this stadium. He says that the wrestling ring is directly above this dungeon.'

'So?' asked Basil. He pointed up at the ceiling. 'It's still solid rock. And it's got to be very thick.'

'Lord Veto put a machine under the wrestling ring to make it go round,' said Bricks. 'Big orcs have to pull levers to turn the wooden cogs, so we had to dig a big hole for all that.'

'Which means,' Jack said, 'all we have to do is smash our way through the ceiling!'

The prisoners looked doubtful.

'Smashing our way through a rock ceiling isn't going to be easy,' said Basil.

'I can do it,' smiled Bricks. 'That's how I got my name. Punching my way through brick walls.'

'And I'm pretty good with rocks,' said Big Rock, grinning.

'But that ceiling is high off the ground,' pointed out Grit.

'That's why we *all* had to get thrown in here,' said Jack. 'Together we can lift up the strongest trolls to burst through the ceiling.'

Basil and Green-Taker looked at Jack, astonished. 'That's brilliant!'

Milo looked at his watch. 'Let's get on with it!'

'Okay!' said Big Rock. 'Trolls, make the bottom!'

Immediately, Taco, Grit, Basil and Green-Taker gripped one another to make a solid platform. Then Robin, Bendy Wendy, Princess Ava, Milo, Jack and George Gnome climbed on top of the trolls and linked arms to make the next level. Carefully, Big Rock and Bricks climbed up the pyramid.

'Watch out down below!' called Bricks. Then the two massive trolls began to punch the ceiling. Bits of broken rock began to fall down.

'Ouch!' said Robin. 'Ow!'

'Not long now!' said Big Rock, and he punched upwards again, and more stones and bricks tumbled down.

A hole had appeared in the ceiling, but Bricks shook his head. 'It's no good!' he groaned. 'There's another layer of bricks and rocks above this one, and it looks even thicker!'

'I guess I just have to accept that my Wrestling Trolls will never wrestle again,' said Milo, slumping down onto the ground.

'GRRAAARRRR!'

The roar filled the dungeon, and the giant figure of Thud reared up from where Jack had been standing on the trolls.

'Thud!' cried Princess Ava. 'Just in time!'

Thud punched both of his giant fists upwards.

'Look out!' yelled Robin in alarm. 'Jump!'

The pyramid suddenly parted down the middle as a massive machine of cogs and pulleys and springs, along with three orcs clinging onto it, came crashing through the ceiling.

As the orcs lay dazed on the ground, Milo pointed upwards at the huge hole that had appeared, from which light and the sound of loud music and shouting was coming. 'Quick!' he shouted. 'Up and out!'

'How?' asked Grit.

'The pyramid!' shouted Ava. 'Only this time, Wendy goes on top. Once she's through, she can haul everyone else up with her arms!'

Once more the trolls linked arms to make the first platform, but this time with Thud and Bricks amongst them. The others clambered

onto the trolls, and then pushed Wendy through the large hole. She swung herself up, and then let down her long arms, which the others used as ropes to climb up.

In the stadium, Lord Veto stood smiling smugly at his team of wrestlers standing together in the ring: Spiderella, Mr Belly, Lightning Rawr, Professor Broccoli, Hardcore, Princess Snuggle, Squarehead, the One-Eyed Gangster, Time-Master and Footballio. The audience was going wild, shouting and chanting.

The chants were getting louder.

'Wrestling Trolls! Wrestling Trolls! We want Wrestling Trolls!'

Lord Veto stepped into the ring with a wide smile, and approached the referee.

'My esteemed opponents don't seem to be coming,' he said. 'I think you must –'

'Here we are!' shouted Milo, shaking the dust out of his hair. He clambered up into the ring.

Lord Veto's mouth dropped open as Big Rock, Grit, Taco Twister, Bendy Wendy, the Masked

Avenger, the gigantic figure of Thud, then Basil, Bricks and Green-Taker climbed out from under the ring. Then came Meenu, Blaze the phoenix – already glowing brightly – and lastly, Robin the old horse, with George Gnome on his back.

'You lot!' he hissed, glaring angrily at them all. 'You've ruined my Orc-Driven Ring Rotater!'

'No time for all that,' shouted the referee. 'We have a match to start!'

As Milo, Meenu, Robin, George Gnome and Blaze watched their team of wrestlers pull themselves into the ring to join Lord Veto's team, they exchanged smiles of relief and pride.

'We did it!' said Milo.

He looked around the huge stadium – which was packed with people waving placards and foam fingers – and at the huge screens that were on every wall so that no part of the action could be missed. The atmosphere was added to by the merchandising stalls around the outside advertising and selling headbands, autographs for sale, wrestling masks and everything else to do with wrestling. The air was thick with the sweet smell of food from the concessions, the taco stalls and those selling peanuts and popcorn. Through the loudspeakers blasted the rocking theme tune, 'A Little More Wrestling', the words of the song filling the stadium:

A little less calculation, a little more wrestling, please.
All this aspiration is really tiring me.
A little more strength, a little less pie,
A little less love, a little more cry,
Close your eyes and drop your hands, let me hit you . . .

The crowd fell silent as the referee picked up the microphone and said, 'Welcome to the greatest Giant Rumble ever!'

At this, the crowd began to yell and shout and the referee continued, 'The rules are simple. Ten wrestlers from two teams in the ring at the same time. When a wrestler is thrown out of the ring and touches the ground outside the ring, he or she is out. The winner is the last one remaining in the ring!'

The crowd was chanting now, 'Trolls! Trolls!' and 'Veto! Veto!'

'And now . . .' said the referee, as he prepared to give the word to begin.

'Stop!' yelled Lord Veto.

All attention turned to Veto as he climbed into the ring. 'This contest is over before it has begun, and my team have won!'

There were boos and shouts of 'Get lost, Lord Veto!' but Veto stood his ground in the centre of the ring, and the yelling from the audience died down.

Veto smirked. 'The rules are clear: ten wrestlers from each team. My opponents have only *nine*!'

The referee frowned, and then began to count: Big Rock, Grit, Taco Twister, Bendy Wendy, the Masked Avenger, Thud, Basil, Bricks and Green-Taker.

'Nine,' he nodded.

'And me!' shouted Milo desperately. 'I'll make

ten.'

'You can't,' said Lord Veto smugly. 'You're registered as a manager, not a wrestler.'

'Me!' yelled Robin. 'I'll make ten.'

The referee shook his head. 'We can't have horses wrestling,' he said. 'Or phoenixes,' he added quickly as Blaze began to glow.

'This is discrimination!' snorted Robin.

Again, the referee shook his head as Lord Veto's smile grew even bigger.

'Only recognised wrestlers can compete,' said the referee.

'Which means . . .' laughed Lord Veto.

'Which means I can join in,' said a voice from the crowd. And a large troll got out of his seat and headed for the ring.

'Goodie Goodie Gumdrops!' yelled Grit delightedly. 'I didn't know you were here!'

'I only came to watch,' smiled Gumdrops. 'But now I'm here, I might as well join in.'

The referee smiled. 'We recognise Goodie Goodie Gumdrops, the Wrestling Troll!' his voice boomed out from the loudspeakers. 'Let the Giant Rumble begin!'

'I protest!' squawked Lord Veto.

'Protest all you want,' snapped the Masked Avenger, and she grabbed Lord Veto by the arm and threw him out of the ring. As he hit the ground she added, 'You're out!' and the crowd erupted into laughter.

Then the bell sounded, and the inside of the ring became a heaving mass of bodies as the twenty wrestlers got to grips with one another. They threw; they gripped; they twisted.

Professor Broccoli was the first one to be thrown out of the ring by Taco Twister, who smiled down on his fallen opponent and said, 'I hate broccoli!' But barely were the words out of his mouth, when Hardcore and Squarehead, working together, had each grabbed one of Taco's arms and hurled him out of the ring.

'Two down!' yelled the crowd.

The battle raged, and more wrestlers were either thrown out, or fell through the ropes and landed on the ringside to be counted out: Goodie Goodie Gumdrops got the One-Eyed Gangster, but Hardcore shoved Bendy Wendy over the ropes. Mr Belly pushed Goodie while Basil bodyslammed Hardcore outside the ring. Bricks chucked out Lightning Rawr, and then Green-Taker sacrificed himself to drag Squarehead out. The Masked Avenger tossed out the snivelling Princess Snuggle, but then Snuggle cheated and grabbed Grit's legs, trying to pull her out. Soon it became a tug of war, with Basil and Bricks trying to keep Grit in, and all of Veto's wrestlers trying to pull her out.

With a great shout from Veto, 'Destroy them!' his team yanked all three of the Wrestling Trolls out.

'We're counting on you, Thud!' shouted Meenu.

Thud grunted and threw himself in a flying head-first dive at Footballio and Time-Master. But as he hurled them through the ropes, they hung onto his arms, and managed to haul Thud with them to crash onto the ground outside the ring.

'Oh no!' said Blaze the phoenix. 'Who's left?'

It all came down to these four wrestlers: Mr Belly, the Masked Avenger, Spiderella and Big Rock.

Remembering what had happened to him the last time he'd come up against Spiderella, Big Rock was wary. Spiderella smiled at him and flicked one of her spiders at the big troll. Big Rock dodged to one side and batted the spider away.

'Scared of spiders, big boy?' taunted Spiderella. She was about to throw another spider at Big Rock when the Masked Avenger somersaulted across the ring and grabbed Spiderella in a lock between her feet, and spun her round, then crashed her to the canvas.

'Hurrah!' shouted the crowd.

But before the Masked Avenger could push Spiderella through the ropes, Mr Belly reacted. He swung his long moustaches, lopping them round the Masked Avenger like ropes, pinioning her arms to her side.

'Finish her, Spiderella!' yelled Mr Belly.

Spiderella scrambled to her feet and threw

herself at the Masked Avenger, her hands grabbing at the Avenger's mask.

'Now we'll see who you really are!' she hissed.

THUMP, THUMP, THUMP!

There was a blur and gasps of astonishment from the crowd as Big Rock slid across the canvas of the ring at a speed that no one expected from the big troll.

BAM!!

His feet smacked into Spiderella and Mr Belly and sent them both tumbling through the ropes. Big Rock reached out to grab the Masked Avenger's hand to stop her going through as well, but he was too late. As Mr Belly fell, his moustaches curled around the Masked Avenger and pulled her beneath the ropes, and all three fell into a heap outside the ring.

'Big Rock!'

The shout went up as the big troll pushed himself to his feet and looked apologetically down at the Masked Avenger.

'I'm sorry,' he said.

'Don't be!' smiled the Avenger. 'We won! You're the last one standing!'

As the roar shouting Big Rock's name echoed all the way round the stadium, Milo strode over to Lord Veto.

'Looks like you lost!' grinned Milo. 'That means YOU have to give up wrestling forever.'

Lord Veto scowled, his face going red and then white with anger. 'You haven't seen the last of me.'

And he turned on his heel and stomped off to shout at his defeated wrestlers.

'One to us!' smiled Jack, who had changed back into his small self again without being seen because everyone's attention had been on the action in the ring. He and Milo looked up at Big Rock, who was parading around the ring, his fists held above his head, acknowledging the roars of the crowd.

Robin looked at the angry Lord Veto as he pushed his beaten wrestlers aside in his haste to get out of the stadium.

'He'll never give up,' grunted Robin. 'He'll just cheat more next time.'

'I know,' replied Milo. 'But in the meantime, we are the Champions! And the Champion of Champions is . . .

BIG ROCK!!'

The Story Adventurers

These children and schools all had ideas included in this book, after participating in www.thestoryadventure.com. Jim wrote a new chapter every Monday, then asked for various suggestions and activities. He picked his favourite ideas and included them in the next chapter. Visit www.thestoryadventure.com to see if there is a new adventure that you can help with right now!

Chapter Two
Burnt Chocolate, Fancyfootball, guava6, Isapop, Izthewiz, Jedi 1, Little Boot, London 2012, McCod, Minim, ninja hamster, spacekids, That-Creative-Boy, Twinkle

Chapter Three

Burnt Chocolate, Fancyfootball, Isapop, Izthewiz, Jedi 1, Lapford Writers, Little Boot, London 2012, Twinkle

Chapter Four

CoolCookie, Doodleduck, Fancyfootball, guava6, Isapop, Little Boot, That-Creative-Boy

Chapter Five

Booty, CoolCookie, Doodleduck, Fancyfootball, Guava6, Izthewiz, London 2012, Minim, Sunshine, Twinkle

Chapter Six

Bunny1, Cheesytoes, Doodleduck, Fancyfootball, Jellynose, Lapford Writers, Little Boot, McCod, Space kids, Squgiggly, St Joseph's Juniors, Strawberry 4, Sunshine, TeenyWeenyHC, Twinkle

Chapter Seven

Booty, Burnt Chocolate, Cool Cookie, Cool Cookie, Fancyfootball, Fancyfootball, Google, Izthewiz, Jellynose, Lapford Writers, Little Boot, London 2012, Miss Funface, Ninja hamster, SausageFingers, St Joseph's Juniors,

Strawberry 4, Sunshine, That-Creative-Boy

Chaper Eight

Cool Cookie, Fancy Football, Google, Izthewiz, Jellynose, Miss Funface, Sourpuss, Strawberry 4, Sunshine, That Creative Boy, Twinkle

Chapter Nine

Booty, Burnt Chocolate, Cool Cookie, Doodleduck, Fancyfootball, guava6, Guava6, Isapop, Izthewiz, Jellynose, Lapford Writers, Little Boot, London2012, spacekids, Strawberry 4, That Creative Boy

Chapter Ten

Burnt Chocolate, Cool Cookie, Doodleduck, Fancyfootball, Google, Guava6, Isapop, Izthewiz, Lapford Writers, Little Boot, Spacekids, Sunshine, That Creative Boy, Twinkle

The Star List

This special list is for those that the Evil Editor deemed worthy of receiving the Star badge, because of particularly good creativity, kindness or thoroughness when participating in www.thestoryadventure.com.

Little Boot and Sunshine, Guava 6, IzTheWiz, That Creative Boy, Burnt Chocolate, Doodleduck, Cool Cookie, Lapford Writers, St Joseph's Juniors, Miss Funface, Strawberries, Jellynose, FancyFootball, Google